MW01593117

AN AGREEABLE MAN

By Nancy Baker

Table of Contents

Dedication

This book is dedicated to my husband, Bill, who makes me happy every day. Thank you for honoring my creativity and for bringing the fruits of my labor into being with your love and support. You are AWESOME!

Acknowledgements

My family has been incredibly supportive during the long time it took to get this book written, and I thank each of them for that. Of special mention is my cousin Shirley who characterized the book as a "candidate for the Christian market." Until then, my book had been difficult to promote, as it dealt with the dark side of the human condition. I began looking for a Christian publisher and found Xulon Press. Publishing Consultant Rene Compton sent me an email that began "It was a pleasure speaking with you today and hearing what God had placed on your heart to write." My Xulon publication team, under the leadership of Rochelle Colon and Sabrina Johnson, has been so easy to work with. Editor Amy Sleper gave me a much-needed boost with her insightful editorial comments and her suggestions for improvement. Model for comic relief hairdresser *extraordinaire,* Lucille le Vale, was found within our extended family, as was the character of Brian whose personal traits embody those looked for in FBI Agents. Special thanks goes to the receptionists and kennel staff at our local Animal Medical Center for their loving care of our dog Jackson, the model for Lucky Charm.

Introduction

Disclaimer

There is material in the text of An Agreeable Man that may cause flashbacks or painful memories for those people who have experienced the trauma of rape, incest, or betrayal by an authority figure, and other examples of child sex abuse. Those who have sought out or happened upon graphic images on the Internet may be upset and mesmerized at the same time. Real time sex videos are especially upsetting. Your brain and heart may be horrified at what you see and hear. It is difficult to process these situations without professional help. Fortunately, there are resources to help you, starting with your relationship with God through prayer. You will receive guidance if you ask for it, and people will be brought into your life who can help you, if you seek them out.

The genesis of the first draft of this novel came from my desire to write a book in serialized form on my blog www.watchnancybakerwrite.com. I want to thank each of my readers for going along with me, so to speak, when I decided to write An Agreeable Man in this manner. Unorthodox, maybe, but I thought that it would be an interesting exercise in writing for me and perhaps would give my readers the feeling of looking over the writer's shoulder to watch me write. I did not take into account that my creative spirit would be shackled by the restrictions of writing for publication according to a set time.

Thankfully, several of my readers cared, and became my encouragement without being judgmental when I didn't post according to a schedule. Instead, they wanted to know all about my characters and what they were doing—and I wanted to tell them. In my mind, I knew my characters as real people dealing with real issues. I wanted my readers to know that events change us, and that the more we understand each other, the more we can help each other.

But as much as my readers liked the characters in An Agreeable Man, some did not like the issues of child pornography, or the fact that the Catholic Church was involved in such dark issues, or that so much child sex abuse exists in the homes of people that we could possibly know and like—and maybe even in the homes of people very close to us.

This book took its toll on me as a person. Upon the completion of the initial draft, I went into a deep depression after reading and viewing all the research information—books, newspapers, magazines, videos, blogs, web sites, phone calls to the FBI, personal interviews with those who had been abused, and my own personal knowledge. My depression is getting better as time goes on. But the residual effects on kids who are abused will last as long as they live. Thankfully, there are excellent therapists who can be of great help in getting the abused person to recognize triggers and to show them how to respond appropriately. There are medications that will soothe the brain as it struggles with unwanted memories and difficulties in learning.

The situations depicted in this book are true, accurate, and factual. The only creative parts of the book are the storyline and the characters, which I had the utmost pleasure in developing. Thank you for visiting with my characters in this book, and with me.

Nancy Baker lives with her husband and their elderly Jack Russell Terrier "Jackson" (role model for Lucky Charm), south of Nashville Tennessee. She welcomes your comments addressed to nancybaker@comcast.net and invites you to visit her blog www.watchnancybakerwrite.com.

Chapter One

On the way home from the funeral, Merle Evans stopped by the pet store and bought a dog. He was a Scottie puppy, no more than eight inches from his jet black nose to his tiny little tail. The pet-store owner said he had papers, but that his long ears would make him unsuitable for show to prospective owners who planned to show their dogs in competition.

"Unsuitable for show — indeed!" thought Merle. She loved his long ears, and the way his hair parted down the middle of his back, and the way his beady little black eyes stared straight at her, as if awaiting orders.

The clerk packed up the dog bed and the puppy food and toys while Merle held the puppy. She handed the clerk a credit card (which Mr. Evans would *not* have approved of), shifting the fidgeting ball of fur to her left arm while she signed the credit slip with her right hand.

As the clerk loaded the packages into her car, Merle wondered what she would tell the relatives and friends at her house. She couldn't tell them she had just bought a dog; that seemed callous, even to her. The truth was, she had grown tired of sitting on the couch at the funeral home before the service while people filed by her, making remarks intended to be kind, but which came off as kind of banal. She didn't relish the thought of sitting on her own couch at home and hearing the same kind of remarks, while trying to remember who made them. She was in no mood to think of Mr. Evans' death right now. She would do that later, when she was in a better frame of mind.

She needed something to cheer her up, to make her happy, to take her mind off of Mr. Evans' death. It was then that she thought of the puppy. Yesterday, she had driven past the pet shop on her way to the funeral home to finalize arrangements and saw him in the window. He had cocked his head to one side and put his chin on his paws, sphinx-like, and looked calmly at her, as if he knew she would come back to get him. But she was surprised to hear herself say, just as the funeral was over, "Why wait until tomorrow?"

The funeral had been grim. First of all, while she was used to going to church on Sundays, she had never attended a funeral in her life. Jack went to those with his friends, Tom Watkins, Dan Newsome and Bob Roberts. Those four went everywhere together — hunting, fishing, golfing, ball games — and each supported the other when their various charities had events.

Mr. Evans, "Jack", was a banker, a founding member and one of the senior employees in the bank. Tom was in insurance, *"the one-stop-shop insurance agent,"* he liked to say. Dan was in alumni relations for the local university and traveled a lot. Bob was the president of a small company that had international ties. He traveled as well. But they were all here today to honor their friend, Jack Evans.

Bob had been chosen to represent the three friends and he was to speak to the assembled crowd that overflowed into the church's outer rooms, where the attendees would watch the service on closed circuit TV. It had taken sixty three cars to bring them all to the church and the Highway Patrol was out in full force for the trip to the burial plot.

Merle was seated at the front and felt the full force of the aura of the assembled crowd. It pulsated down from the back rows to the front pews and broke over her like crashing waves at a surfboarding event. It overwhelmed her. If only she could close her eyes and sleep through it.

But no. Bob got up with a few papers in his hand and laid them on the pulpit.

"Hi. My name is Bob Roberts and…I have been asked to say a few words on behalf of my friend Jack Evans, who died last Saturday. *Suddenly.*" At this point, the suave world traveler gulped for breath and tried to regain his composure.

"I'm sorry. I really don't know where to begin to tell you what Jack Evans meant to me as my best friend…" He trailed off again, looking down at his notes.

"This is hard. Honestly, I can't begin to tell you how intertwined our lives were. Like, you know, that cartoon character—Bugs Bunny—you know how his long ears wound around each other until it looked like one big tall rabbit ear?" Now the tears started and his face screwed up in a grimace.

He grabbed his notes and said, "I can't do this. Tom, you and Dan will have to take over."

And he sat down, face in his handkerchief, shoulders heaving.

Tom stood up and walked purposefully to the podium. He had no pages in his hand. He faced the packed worship hall.

"Jack Evans was my best friend. And I'll bet you will hear that over and over today, because if Jack took you as a friend, you became like family. Jack had a lot of friends. And there was nothing that Jack wouldn't do for any one of us. He was loyal to a fault. He was the type of man who would give to those less fortunate than he was without even thinking about it. He always counted his blessings, and encouraged us to look at what we had going for us instead of what we lacked. He changed me from a borderline depressed person into an optimistic person who now tries to find the positive in every person and every situation. Thank you, Jack."

He walked back to his seat, grim-faced.

Dan got up and slowly walked to the podium. Tall, lanky, with a burst of reddish hair that looked like it had been slept on, he turned to face the crowd.

"Well, this is the hardest thing I've ever had to do. Thank you all for coming to honor our friend, Jack Evans. Jack would probably be embarrassed at this great turnout.

"I loved a good crowd when I played basketball, and later when the joints began to act up a bit, the four of us would play 'pick-up' basketball. I remember the first time we played. What should have been an easy win for me, being a foot taller than Jack, turned into the hardest game of my life. He was determined to give me a run for my money. Jack was never afraid to go after what he wanted no matter how hard he had to work for it. I racked up the most points, but Jack taught me how to win in the Game of Life."

He started to say something else, but thought better of it and silently ambled back to his seat.

Then it was the minister's turn to talk about Jack. How he contributed to so many charities, not only money but also volunteer work, inspiring others to volunteer as well. How he helped build the new hospital, and a kitchen/sleep wing in the Family Activities section of the church to feed and care for the homeless; and how you could always count on Jack Evans for advice, money, volunteers or whatever was needed to enrich the town he so loved.

Merle was not mentioned once. For all the world knew, Jack Evans was a bachelor.

She did not recognize the man whose funeral she had attended by the words she had heard spoken. Could there have been two funerals at the same time for two men named Jack Evans? *I am losing my mind,* she thought. That would have given her cause to panic, if she hadn't been so very tired. She needed to get out of there before the crush of people came over to her to offer condolences. But since she had not even been acknowledged as Jack's wife in the funeral eulogies, why should she stay?

It made perfect sense to her to stand up at the end of the funeral and walk to her car, announcing to no one in particular "Go on to the house—I'll be there shortly." Everyone nodded and whispered "Poor thing, it's just beginning to sink in…" and "She needs to grieve in private…" and "Some fresh air is just what she needs…" (Actually, it never occurred to her that she should be grieving. She felt a cautious sense of freedom, as if a prison door had been carelessly left open. Should she make a run for it? *Hurry, before they come back and close the door!*)

So, now what? Here she was, back from who knows where, with a puppy in her arms. How would she smuggle the puppy into the house? She had to think, to make a plan. Mr. Evans usually made all the plans, but he wasn't here now, was he? It was up to her to work this out.

Chapter Two

Her brain felt dusty, cobwebby. But the puppy moved in her arms and she was instantly overcome with an emotion so strong, it caused her to gasp. Eyes shining, she weighed her options. She could walk in boldly and say to everyone, "This is my dog—*whatshisname*". (…what *was* his name? She couldn't quite remember.) But she didn't want to take the direct approach. Years of having to deal indirectly with Jack Evans had made her a master of the cautious move. She would park her car in the back alley and walk the fifty or so feet to the back porch, through the bathroom, and enter their bedroom—*her* bedroom now! She then would put the puppy in his bed and close the door. He would probably sleep until all the company left.

As she entered the dining room from the hallway, she overheard someone talking in the living room. "Poor Merlie, wonder who will take care of her? You know, Jack did everything, even paid the bills. He took her shopping, wrote the checks, helped put up the groceries…"

"Well, I heard she never learned to drive, being raised in an orphanage. You've got to admit she is a good cook and she keeps a spotless house. Not a looker, but a good woman and a good wife to Jack."

Merlie felt as if she had been slapped. *Not a looker –?* She glanced at her face in the mirror above the sideboard, putting her hands to her cheeks. No, sadly, she was not a looker. Somehow, the finality of it numbed her and she felt like she was slogging through molasses, waist high. It was such an effort just to walk into that room and keep a civil tongue. But Jack was a stickler for good manners, so she pasted on a small smile and went in to greet her guests.

The spacious living room/dining room area was filled with about twenty-five people, roughly the size of Jack's annual Christmas party. And the same people were there, Jack's closest friends and those community leaders whose projects he supported with his time, money, and his presence throughout the year. A few of them brought their families. Merle had no idea how to entertain small children, having none of her own.

Some of the nuns from St. Paul the Servant Orphanage were there. Merle realized that the Mother Superior was talking to her, but her vocal sounds didn't match up with her lip movements, and Merle couldn't understand the content because of the time lag. "*Like a bad TV program,*" she thought. Oh, how she wished that *her* Mother Superior could be here. She would know how to get Merle through this mess. And Merle could "confess her sins" and feel God's forgiveness and redemption and grace. But Merle had never met *this* Mother Superior, although she had been at the helm of the local orphanage for at least six years.

"How are you holding up, Mrs. Evans?" Merle understood that question. But what do I say, she thought? How can I lie to a NUN? No problem, as it turned out. The four nuns surrounded her, three with their hands on her back and shoulders, and Mother Superior's hands holding hers, and they began chanting a prayer for her healing.

Everyone stopped talking and turned their heads in Merle's direction. There was an awkward silence when the chanting was over and the look on everyone's faces asked the same question, "Do we clap; resume talking as if nothing had happened; or exit the room?" The nuns made it easy for them, as they filed out of the room and out of the house, their duty having been met.

Merle scouted the room with her eyes and found the person she was looking for, Brian Malley. Brian had been hired by Jack to be a handyman of sorts, to keep the yard mowed, the cars running smoothly, put light bulbs where needed inside the house. Jack had told Merle that Brian owned a small engine repair shop that had quickly spread into doing all the small jobs that an absentee homeowner couldn't do or didn't want to do. An ex-Navy man, Brian vowed that his future would be determined by working with his hands, not with a weapon.

He would be forever grateful to the Navy, therefore, that he had served long enough to have his education paid for at the local university. He was taking a few computer courses until he could decide on a major.

Jack had hired Brian after a telephone interview, but Brian had never met him. Lately, he had been getting to know Merle better, because he would tell her about his classes and had figured out that she was desperate to get a degree herself. The most intimate conversation they had had to date was when she told him about Jack's comment that she didn't need to go to college since "it wouldn't do you any good." Merle had come close to tears, telling Brian about it, and Brian almost put his arm around her shoulders to comfort her. Somehow, he felt that Jack would not like for Merle, or any other of his possessions, to be touched by someone else.

But today, he came to see whether Merle would continue to need his services, or not. He didn't know what her plans were, but he was sure he could take a lot of man's work off her "to do" list, and maybe help in some new ways as well.

"Mrs. Evans, I am so sorry for your loss. I never met Mr. Evans in person, but I know he was well respected in the community. I heard his friends and the minister talking about him…"

Merle raised her head and looked into his eyes. Softly, she spoke. "Tell me, Brian, did you also hear anything said about his *wife*? About *me*? If you hadn't known better, would you have thought that the wonderful Mr. Evans even *had* a wife?" Her voice shook as she struggled to keep her anger from showing.

Brian leaned toward her and put his hand lightly on her shoulder, but the steel of his fingers dug into her flesh and shocked her into control. To an onlooker, he was offering a sympathetic touch, but he was not offering sympathy when he said in a low voice, "Get a hold of yourself, Mrs. Evans. Stand straight. Don't let them see you cry."

In a louder voice, he said, "Our contract runs until the end of the year, and I am assuming that will still be in effect. I will be here next week, regular time, but I want you to call me and let me know when to come this week, okay?" He handed her his business card with his business phone and his cell phone numbers on it. And quietly, he leaned toward her again and said, "Call me any time, night or day, for any reason. Please?"

She stiffened and, taking his card, she thanked him and said, "Go ahead and come regular time this week and I will let you know when to come next week. And Brian—thanks."

Some of the guests were leaving, but Frances, her next-door neighbor, stayed to help.

"You look tired, dear. Why don't you go lie down and try to rest? I'll clean up and load your dishwasher before I go home."

Merle allowed herself a few tears. Of course everyone thought she finally was realizing that Jack was gone, and they began to leave out of deference to her feelings. It came as a surprise to Merle that *anger* could cause such a flow of tears and emotion.

Merle wiped her eyes with one of the lace-edged handkerchiefs Jack's sister had sent her for Christmas last year, the Christmas they gave Jack the portable CD player and a dozen CDs. Merle loved the jazz recordings, but Jack convinced her that learning to operate the CD player was just too difficult 'for a woman.' He did offer to put on any CD she might want to hear, but since he worked, he was never around when she wanted to hear the music.

Merle didn't want to think about Jack just yet. But the thoughts kept coming, in a random and meaningless whirl. Helplessly, Merle listened to her brain as it chattered away about Jack.

Jack was an early riser. He had told Merle that he had been raised in the orphanage here in Duchess and had chores to do before breakfast, even as a young boy. After leaving the orphanage, he went to the local university and, with his first degree, got a job at the local bank — first as a gofer, then a clerk, then rising to Vice President of Marketing. Finally, he was asked to help establish a new bank in town, and he took the opportunity. He prided himself on being the first to learn a new thing, and was the undisputed master of his area of work and his home life.

"Who cares? Who cares one iota what Jack did. He's dead. He won't be doing anything any more." Merle put her hands to her ears.

Jack began to work with young people in his church, and spent hours teaching them about business and his hobbies of stamp collecting, hunting, and fly-fishing. He made all his own lures and knew just where, and when, the fish were biting. He spent evenings in his home office with his stamp collections, and Saturdays fishing or hunting with his friends. Sundays he taught Sunday School and served as a deacon in the Methodist Church. (After they got married, Merle wanted to sing in the choir, but Jack was firm in his belief that a deacon should have his Missus at his side.)

"Shut up! I don't want to hear any more about Jack..." Merle stood up and walked toward the kitchen.

The house was quiet now; everybody was gone.

Merle heard a strange noise and then a series of very aggressive small – *barks?* Instantly her mood and her heartbeat elevated! She, Merle Evans, had a dog! She had almost forgotten about the puppy until she heard him yipping behind the bedroom door. She ran to open it, and fell to her knees, scooping him up and hugging him to her.

"You don't care if I'm not a 'looker', do you? They said you were 'unsuitable for show' and you are the *most beautiful thing in the world* to me." She held the puppy up to her shoulder and went to the kitchen to warm up some milk. His tiny tongue licked her cheek.

As she walked through the dining room, she glanced at her reflection in the mirror. Who was *this* person, holding that precious puppy? Whoever she was, she was *beautiful*! Her cheeks were rosy, eyes shiny, hair loose and free! She looked happy, even with traces of tears down her cheeks.

She held the puppy in both hands, arms straight up. "It's because of *you*! You are my good luck charm!" That was when the idea came to her to name the puppy Lucky Charm.

Mr. Evans didn't believe in luck. For years Merle had sent in the sweepstakes entries that flooded their mailbox, and she steadfastly believed that someday, she would win and win big. She could win five million dollars this week if she had the lucky number she sent in last time. Mr. Evans said that playing the sweepstakes was no different from gambling, no different from the lottery. Merle agreed that gambling was wrong, but somehow winning the sweepstakes seemed to be the result of perseverance and of paying attention to the details. It took a lot of time to follow all those directions, especially if you weren't buying anything.

One of the worst arguments she and Mr. Evans ever had was over her buying *Reader's Choice* books from the sweepstakes stamp sheets. "It's wasted money, and I'll not pay for another book," he fumed. It took him by surprise when she stood up to him and told him that *reading* was her hobby, and seeing as how he was always saying that she should *have* a hobby, well now she *had* one, and she had to have *books* in order to *read*. He went into his home office and shut the door. They never spoke of it again.

Chapter Three

66 Guess what, Lucky Charm. I can order all the books I want to now..." Merle paused. Money. That's what she was thinking about now. Do you suppose that was what Tom Watkins wanted to talk about when he asked her to come to his office some time next week? She knew Mr. Evans had good insurance. Mr. Evans used to tell people he was 'insurance poor'. Somehow she had never thought about profiting from his death. Oh, my — what an *"embarrassment of riches"*, as her Aunt Leora would say.

Freedom and money too, Merle thought.

"This calls for more planning, Lucky. What do you think we should do with our insurance money? Travel? Take a cruise? Buy new clothes? Buy a new *face*?" She almost stopped breathing just thinking about the possibilities.

She sat down at the kitchen table and put Lucky on a placemat facing her. She had to think about this. Mr. Evans was quite the ladies man. Everyone said so, but in a nice way, of course.

He was such an *agreeable* man. Mannerly. Reasonable. Pleasant. He enjoyed the attention, yet managed to maintain the respect of all. Merle wasn't jealous and she used to wonder why until one day it dawned on her. Jack was a *surface* person. He had no depth of feeling. He had never required very much of her, and had given very little of himself in return. It was so simple; she was amazed she hadn't figured it out before now.

When they were first married, she wanted to take some courses at the local university, but he was adamant in his refusal. She didn't need to know any more stuff, he said. It wouldn't do her any good. (Why couldn't he have said she was perfect just the way she was? Or that he was satisfied with her in every way? Anything except 'it won't do you any good.') When he refused to talk about it any more, she prostrated herself on the kitchen floor, sobbing, desperate for him to understand her need to learn, or at least, not understanding, desperate for him to comfort her. He did neither. After a brief moment of looking down at her, he stepped over her body and walked out the kitchen door. Two hours later, he came back, read the paper in his chair by the fireplace, and went to bed, punctually, at 10:00.

Jack's activities set the timetable of their lives. He never told her what was required of her, what he expected, but she learned to discern his needs and wants by watching his body language. His swift glance over the meal displayed on the table and the purposeful unfolding of the linen (never paper) napkin was tacit approval. If he ever so slightly raised his 'pointer' finger toward something, he wanted it passed to him. Heaven forbid he should ever say 'Fine meal, Merle, but I wouldn't want to eat this every day.' That was the same as saying "Never serve this again in this house." To his credit, he did say *please* and *thank you* about most things.

Jack paid all the bills and gave her a small weekly allowance, pin money he called it. She never had enough to buy anything that required any anticipation. She had to ask him for everything she bought, and if she was brave enough to *really* want something, like that green brocade chair, she had to ask—no, *beg*—more than once.

She had seen the chair in the window at *Simmons Fine Furnishings*. It was soft green brocade with a fluted back and delicately rolled arms. It was a *lady's* chair. She knew she would *feel* like a lady sitting in it. For the first time in a long time, she wanted something so badly that she risked asking for it.

"Jack," she ventured, when he got home that night. "I found a chair that I think we should buy. It's at *Simmons* and it's only seventy-five dollars."

"Is that with or without tax?" he said.

Head spinning, she stammered, "I'm not sure. But I can find out." She was so excited! He actually seemed to be entertaining the thought of buying the chair!

That night for supper she made his favorite meal—twice-stuffed potatoes with pork loin medallions and green beans—and baked a French Silk Chocolate Pie with extra meringue for dessert. He complimented her, not once, but twice on the excellent supper.

Elated, she set out the next morning for *Simmons*. The chair was $82.50 with tax, and she told Mr. Simmons himself that he should put the chair "on hold" for her.

That night when Jack came home, she told him the price of the chair. "Well, we'll see." He opened his paper and held it up, covering his face from her view—a sign he didn't want to be disturbed.

"Jack, I've already told Mr. Simmons to hold the chair for us until I could tell you the price. So if you'll write the check, I'll take it in tomorrow and have the chair delivered..."

She got no further. The paper slowly lowered until a red-faced Mr. Evans could be seen. "You what?"

Then he went to the phone and dialed Mr. Simmons at home and told him that he should put the chair back on the show-room floor. *Merlie* had gotten it all wrong, as usual, he said. They didn't need any extra furniture, not with just the two of them, he said. He was sorry that *Merlie* had caused Mr. Simmons the inconvenience of holding a chair without consulting him about the matter, but he could assure Mr. Simmons that it wouldn't happen again. "We've had a little talk on the matter," he said, and he hung up.

Merle was stunned. She walked slowly to the kitchen and sat down at the table. This was the chair that she could feel like a *Lady* in. This was a chair she could feel *important* in. This was a chair that she could *entertain company* in. ("Oh, please, take the green brocade chair, it's for company.")

She felt drained, leaden, so tired.

After that, she decided that life would be easier if she just concentrated on what Mr. Evans wanted and forgot about what she wanted. In fact, life would be easier if she forgot that she wanted anything at all.

And for a while, life *was* easier.

Chapter Four

Merle had been giving Jack the "silent treatment". But Jack had not noticed, because he interpreted her silence as assent. In other words, whatever Jack wanted done, Merle did, with no discussion, no back talk. And Jack didn't miss this important element in their relationship. But the mind does not go silent, as Merle found out. It continues to listen, and take in what is said, and agree or disagree, and it begins to plan…

It was remarkably simple just to go inside yourself, she learned. At the beginning of Lent, the minister had talked about the things that one could give up as a test of being 'in the world, but not of the world.' She decided to give up *speaking* except when absolutely necessary. The stock phrases she used with Jack didn't count as talking.

She had no friends to chat with. Jack's standards for friends were remarkably high. He, of course, was friends with everyone. How they praised him, and how they told her she must be so proud to be married to Jack, friend to all, *wonderful* Jack. She just smiled, a smile she had practiced in front of the mirror until she got the tilt of the lips just right, no teeth showing, eyes crinkling in the corners, in such a pleasant manner.

As long as Jack kept to his schedule, life was bearable. She heard the alarm each morning, shook his shoulder, and went to the kitchen to fix his breakfast. They ate together at the kitchen table. There was always the standard question — "What do you have planned today?" — which she answered with a brief list of household chores. Monday there was the wash to do; Tuesday she vacuumed and dusted; Wednesday she polished the wood surfaces in the public rooms of the house; Thursday (coupon day) she bought groceries; and Friday she handled whatever correspondence or calls needed a response. Saturday they ate breakfast out, same place, same time, same meal. Then, as Jack liked to tell people, they each had their 'free time'. From 9:00 a.m. until 5:00 p.m., they went their separate ways. Sunday, of course, was spent at Church.

First there was Sunday School, often preceded by a breakfast of some sort in the church's dining area, always followed by the church service itself. They sat in the same pew, heard the same sermon from the same minister. Jack loved the regularity of it, but it was too much idle time for Merle; it gave her time to think, and thinking was dangerous.

It wouldn't have been so bad if she hadn't loved books so much. It was her one luxury; actually, she considered books a necessity. But the more she read, the more she realized how different life was for other people, and she came to want a different life for herself. How to accomplish this was food for thought, indeed.

It was odd that the answer to this mental rebellion should come to her in church.

The minister was talking about Eve being told by the serpent to pluck a fruit (thought to be an apple) from the Tree of Life and tempt Adam with it. Idly she thought, "An apple a day keeps the doctor away." But that didn't exactly relate to what the minister was saying. Yet, it reminded her of something. Ah, yes. *Apples.* Jack was very allergic to apples. In fact, it was second nature for her to minutely examine the labels on every can, bag, and box to make sure there were no hidden apple bits in them. Just yesterday, she had read how applesauce could be substituted for butter or margarine in a recipe for muffins. It made them moist, but the other ingredients hid the apple flavor. That could be dangerous because Jack would never smell or taste such a hidden ingredient. Or would he?

She decided to find out.

The next day was Monday, and as she did the wash, she thought about apples. By Thursday, she had made a plan.

To Merle's knowledge, no one knew about Jack's allergy. He had hated admitting it to her; he thought having an allergy was a sign of weakness. But he had to tell her since she did all the cooking, and there was no more said about the matter.

The following Saturday, Merle told Jack that she was going to be baking all day and that he was not to come into her kitchen. She would have some of those delicious banana-nut muffins he so enjoyed for Sunday morning breakfast, and then fresh bread with homemade soup for lunch. Jack left in a great mood to go fishing with his friends, and Merle began to bake.

Hours later, she looked at the kitchen counter covered with muffins, loaves of bread, a cake and two pies. Except for the bread, all had applesauce in them.

As Jack came in the back door, he picked up a muffin and took the hot cocoa Merle offered him. "This smells good," he said, and reached for another muffin as he sat down.

How pleasant he looks, Merle thought. There was a big smile on his face. He was licking his fingers as he stretched out, filling the recliner so nicely. Such an *agreeable* man.

She watched him out of the corner of her eye as she cleaned up the mess in the kitchen. He was reading the paper, as he always did after he came in from fishing. Everything seemed normal, and yet…

He's dozed off, she thought. He must be asleep. He hasn't turned any pages in several minutes; hasn't read anything to her from the paper; hasn't asked for more hot chocolate. She wiped her hands on her apron and walked around the counter to his chair.

"Jack?" She leaned down as she turned his recliner toward her. Then she saw his face, bug-eyed and slowly turning purple. She hesitantly placed two fingers on his wrist. There was no pulse.

It appeared that Jack Evans was dead.

Merle sat back on the couch, dazed. It was all too easy. Applesauce and muffins. She had killed him with *applesauce and muffins*.

Maybe he wasn't dead, but just silently choking, or in a coma, or God knows what. She had to get help!

She picked up the phone and dialed 911. It seemed forever before the police desk clerk asked how he could help. She was still holding the phone in one hand and the dishtowel in the other hand when the policeman rang the doorbell.

After ascertaining that Mr. Evans was really dead, the policeman called for an ambulance and then asked Merle some questions, filling out his forms as she answered them. As if from a distance, she watched this scenario, looking down on Jack, dead in his favorite chair, and herself being questioned by a policeman.

She wondered when would be the appropriate time to confess. The policeman might not believe her. She hardly believed it herself. Who would have thought you could kill someone with *applesauce*?

In response to the officer's suggestion, Merle called her next-door neighbor and more or less let her take over. She realized that she must be in some kind of shock. She heard things people asked her and replied to them, but she had not the slightest idea what was said. It was as if she had no more memory. It made her uncomfortable that other people were in her house, uninvited by her; yet she had gone over to other people's homes when there was a death, had taken food, had asked the same standard questions. She knew the drill. She just didn't like being on the other end of it.

She excused herself to go to the bathroom, and as she passed the kitchen door, she heard the policeman calling in his final report.

"Looks like an open and shut case to me. He came in from fishing, the wife had been baking and gave him some hot chocolate and muffins, and after he ate them, he died. I suppose of natural causes. He might have choked on one of the muffins. His eyes are all popped out. But she said he didn't make a sound because he was reading his paper. I've collected the mug he drank out of, and one of the muffins from the same batch he got his from, but I don't think the lab boys will find anything suspicious. His old lady is in shock. She just sits and looks off in the distance. I got her next-door neighbor in here and she has called in the relatives, so I'm on my way back to the precinct. Looks pretty straightforward to me."

Merle stood glued to the floor. It never occurred to her that she might *not* have to confess to murder. Or that she might *not* have to go to trial and say bad things about Jack, about how he had such a rich and full life with friends and activities and purpose, and how she had nothing to compare with that, and now he's dead and she's still alive, and who's the lucky one now?

Chapter Five

The day after the funeral, her neighbor Frances called. Merle answered on the third ring.

"Did I wake you?" Merle glanced at the clock and noted that it was 7:00 a.m.

"No, I've already been up, regular time." She didn't tell Frances that she was trying to establish a schedule for Lucky Charm and so she was observing when her puppy wanted to eat, to go outside, to sleep and to play. It seemed that Lucky would be an early riser, and was famished after the night's sleep. He had eaten a third of a can of dog food, and would have eaten more, but Merle decided not to overfeed him. She had already taken him out in the back yard and let him have the run of the fenced in area. She had laughed her head off to see him sniff his way around the perimeter of the yard, peeing as he went. "What is he doing?" she wondered, and then she giggled as she answered herself, "He's checking his p-mails." No, staid old Frances might not think that was funny.

"Well, I just called to see if you needed any help in writing Jack's obituary", Frances said.

"No, I left that up to Donovan, Jack's assistant at the bank. He called last night and offered to do it, and since he had been with Jack for so long, he surely knows more about him than I do. So I was grateful for his offer. He's going to stop by this morning and show me the rough draft and will take it to the newspaper later on today."

"Oh — well, what newspapers are you going to put it in?"

"I guess just the local paper, *The Duchess Daily News*. Should it go anywhere else?"

"I thought it might go to his university paper and to *The Illinois Challenger*, the state capital banking newspaper but I am sure that Donovan will have all the distribution sites covered. Well, Merlie, if there is anything I can do, please just ask."

Merle gritted her teeth and said, "Well, actually Frances, there is one major thing. Please stop calling me *Merlie*. That was Jack's little verbal game with my name and I hated it. Just call me *Merle*, please."

Frances was taken aback. Never had she heard Merle even raise her voice, and she certainly had never heard Merle speak a single word against Mr. Evans. Mercy! It must be all the upsetting events that had loosened her tongue.

After Frances rang off, Merle wondered just how proactive she should be in these after-funeral obligations. She didn't even know what they were. Oh—well maybe Donovan could fill her in. He had been most helpful in arranging Jack's wedding and honeymoon, and every Christmas he chose the guest list for their annual Christmas party, sent out the invitations, and helped by choosing the menu and the caterers. He also drew up their Christmas gift list and kept up with the birthdays of the important people that Jack knew, sending cards and sometimes gifts. Merle knew this because of so many people thanking *her* as they saw her at church or the grocery store or the beauty parlor. But it had all been Donovan's doing.

Suddenly, a thought came to her, who would Donovan work for, now that Jack was gone?

Oh dear—she just remembered. When Donovan called about the obituary, she had told him that Jack had no living relatives, but of course, that was not correct. Jack had a sister, Dolores, whom Merle had never met, and only knew of because of the Christmas presents that came each year. Gorgeous presents for Jack. And cheap ones for Merle. It had hurt the first two or three Christmases, but Jack told her not to pout over it because he and his sister had a special bond, being orphans. "But, Jack." she had said. "I'm an orphan, too. Don't you remember?"

It was one of the few times that Jack expressed kindness to her with a brief hug, and a gruff "I remember".

The phone rang again, more loudly it seemed than the first call.

"Hello? Yes, this is Merle. No, not *Merlie*. Who is this? Oh, hello, Dolores. I'm glad Donovan's phone messages caught up with you. Yes, it all happened so fast, and when we tried to locate you, no one seemed to know where you were, only that you were traveling. Oh, London. How nice. Of course you couldn't break your trip schedule to come back for the funeral. I understand. The what? When is the reading of the will? Well, I don't exactly know just yet. I'm sure Donovan will know and we will let you know then. Okay, bye."

She had barely put the phone back into its base when it rang again.

"Hello? Oh, Donovan, I'm so glad you called. When are you coming over tomorrow? Ten would be fine. See you then. Oh, Oh, wait. Frances wanted to know which papers you were putting the obituary in, and Jack's sister Dolores called, wanting to know when the will is to be read. I told her I didn't know, but that you would…yes, tomorrow at 2:00 p.m. is fine. And where is it? In your office? Okay, I know where that is. See you at ten."

It was a good thing that Lucky was sleeping so soundly, snoring in fact. She went into the spare bedroom, now Lucky's room, and found him lying on his back in his new bed, all four paws in the air, snoring away. Let sleeping dogs lie, she thought.

Merle didn't have much of a past to remember outside of the St. Rose of Guadalupe orphanage in Duquesne, just a few miles from Duchess. She had never been told who her parents were, or what horrendous event had happened that they never came to see her. Their names were never mentioned, even in the nightly prayers at the orphanage. Just the words, "Bless my parents who gave me earthly Life, O Jesus Christ, who gives me Life Eternal."

Merle had been saved from the sorrow and disgrace of having no parents by the loving care of her Mother Superior, Sister Mary Angeline. Under her tutelage, she progressed through the school system and was able to graduate high school at age eighteen. She considered the nun to be her true mother and she flourished under the watchful, and proud, eye of the woman who was her friend as well.

Merle had been deemed worthy of learning cooking and domestic skills, in preparation to take care of a house for someone in the future as a housekeeper, or for a husband, should she marry.

And marry she did, to the man who had started visiting her at the orphanage when Merle was sixteen, and who proposed to her when she was eighteen. The nuns were deliriously happy at this outcome because Merle was one of the more docile and obedient orphans, not inclined to have the initiative to estab-lish herself as a worker who could live on her own. And as it turned out, the orphanage came into a tidy nest egg from Jack, which he referred to as "Merlie's dowry."

Merle was just grateful to Jack for taking her out of the orphanage. She idolized him as if he were her own Jesus Christ—Savior, Protector, Encourager, Partner, and Friend. His visits and gifts made her feel special and attractive and worthy of this great man's affection.

Initially, it seemed that the orphanage had prepared Merle in every way for marriage, especially as to the running of a house and the care and feeding of a husband. But no one told Merle about sex. That issue was addressed by the Mother Superior the night before her wedding. She made vague references to "do your duty" and "do whatever your husband tells you to do", but nothing more. Merle definitely came to the marriage bed a virgin.

But that was the second problem. The first problem was that she had never seen a naked adult person, male or female. And the third problem was that she didn't know how to respond to some of the things Jack asked her to do on their honeymoon. Her only resource was the little bit of information that the nuns gave her, and that was no help at all, as it turned out. The information was, "When in doubt, ask yourself 'What would Jesus do?'" And the nuns were appalled when Merle blurted out, "How can that help me? Jesus Christ never got married."

And then there was the drinking, or rather Jack's attempts to get *her* to drink. He kept suggesting every night of their two-week honeymoon that she have a glass, or two, of wine before they went to bed. She refused, saying she didn't like the taste of wine. And when she asked him if he was going to have some wine as well, he said "No." "Then neither will I," she said. "Your precious Jesus Christ liked wine," he said, sarcastically. "In fact, he turned water into wine." "You are correct", said Merle, "but nowhere in the Bible does it say that he *drank* wine."

Needless to say, they were both glad when the honeymoon was over, but for very different reasons. Soon they would be establishing their living arrangements—separate but equal, Merle thought. She had the household chores and he went out and made a living for them. Just like every other married couple, right?

Wrong.

Chapter Six

Merle felt something touch her shoulder. Sitting up to look at the clock, she saw that it was only 5:30 a.m. That was the time she used to get up to fix Jack's breakfast. "Force of habit, I guess," she said and rolled over — to look straight into the jet black eyes of Lucky Charm. Tail wagging, tongue lolling out one side of his mouth, ears up — Lucky Charm was wide awake and ready to play, or eat, or do anything but sleep.

"Okay, you little rat. Mommy wants to sleep some more." She held her hand out for a lick.

Lucky Charm breathed in deeply and…sneezed, right into her outstretched hand.

Dog snot…yuck!

"Do you have to go potty?" she asked, getting up. Lucky Charm turned round and round ecstatically, as if she had crowned him King of the Doggie World.

"Okay. Let's go outside." She put on her slippers and opened the bedroom door. Together they went to the kitchen where Merle opened the back door for him to go out. Thank goodness she had a fenced in back yard and didn't have to dress every time he wanted to go out.

"Let's see what's on the calendar for today. Oh, yes. Donovan is coming over at 10:00 with a draft of Jack's obituary. And then, what?" She looked at a calendar full of meetings that Jack was obligated to go to, some of which required her presence, but none of which were evidence of *her* schedule. She did nothing that Jack did not deem worthy. And then it hit her — she would never have to go to another of Jack's meetings again.

"WOOF."

Oh, right. Lucky Charm was ready to come back inside. And he would be ravenous. That dog ate the most food to be so small.

"All right, come in, come on in. Do you want your *foods*?" And Lucky Charm did his little tail-chasing bit. "This lady is so easy to train," he thought.

After Lucky Charm had wolfed down a third of a can of Blue Bison dog food, Chicken Chunks today, he did his *Tricks for Treats* that Merle was teaching him, and his trick for today was to *roll over*. She made him sit and then lie down and then she tantalized him with his favorite treat by making a circle around his nose while she gently pushed him into following the treat—and rolling over.

You would have thought that Lucky Charm had won the lottery. Merle clapped and squealed and picked him up and danced around with him. "Good boy, Lucky Charm!" she said over and over.

Finally, she put him down on the floor, and a bit dazed, he slowly walked to his bed in the spare bedroom and promptly went to sleep.

Merle knew he would be out for at least an hour, so she took a shower and fixed breakfast. It felt strange to sit at a table for two without someone across from her. Still, she and Jack never talked at breakfast. He just read the paper that he went outside to get, and then asked her what she would be doing today.

Well, guess what? She could ask—and answer—any question *she* wanted to, now. So she said "Merle, what's on the schedule for today?"

"Well, *Merle*, I have someone coming over at 10:00 this morning, and then I am going to…um, eat lunch at that new restaurant in the mall, and then, um…I am going *to get my hair done.*"

This was a day to look forward to. No more 'duty days' where she had to define a topic of work and give a report on how well (or if) she had gotten it done. *Freedom!* Merle jumped up from the table, arms stretched sky high over her head. And it felt good. Not only the idea of an exciting day — of *her* choosing — but also of just *stretching.* Maybe she could benefit from some exercise, something that would make her feel in shape. She would see what exercise options there were in the mall.

At 10:00 on the dot, Donovan rang her doorbell. He didn't know what to expect, but it certainly was not the *Merlie* that he was used to seeing with Jack. This lady was almost pretty, and radiated youth and enthusiasm. He was prepared for a somber reception and discussion of the obituary, but not this.

"Come in, Donovan," Merle said. "Did you bring the obituary?"

"Yes, I did, and you are certainly welcome to make any changes you might want. This is just a draft"

"Oh, I'm sure it will be perfect. Jack always said your work was as close to perfection as a grown man could get."

Donovan blushed. Compliments were unheard of from Jack, but good to hear, even if it was post-mortem.

They went to the breakfast table and Donovan opened his computer. And there it was, on the screen.

"The Obituary of Thomas Jackson Evans, Local Banker and Generous Citizen of Duchess."

Thomas Jackson Evans, age 42, died peacefully at his home Saturday, August 26, 2013 of natural causes. He had just come back from a fishing trip with his three best friends, Tom Watkins, Dan Newsome, and Bob Roberts. His wife, Merlie Evans, was with him when he died. They had no children. Mr. Evans is survived by his sister, Dolores Gordon and her husband, Joseph Gordon of Orlando, FL.

Mr. Evans went to Duchess State University where he received a bachelor's degree in accounting. He then obtained a master's degree in business administration from Duquesne University, and grad-uated from the Graduate School of Banking of the University of Wisconsin.

Mr. Evans served as president and CEO of the First National Bank of Duchess. He was a board member of the Independent Community Banks of America.

A long-time advocate of continuing education, Mr. Evans attended bank investment school at Southern Methodist University. In his later years, he invested in promising young people in high school by ensuring them a paid-for first year at the local university, and if they earned good grades, he guaranteed funding their college years through graduation.

He was a staunch supporter of St. Paul the Servant Orphanage in Duchess, giving time, money, and other resources as needed to ensure the education of the young men and women housed there. Mr. Evans was himself an orphan and came to live in Duchess after completing his high school education.

A long-time member of the United Methodist Church, Mr. Evans taught a unique course for young men on "What Would Jesus Do About...Fishing, or Stamp Collecting, or Camping" or whatever else would allow him to share his faith and his passions (hobbies). Mr. Evans was skilled at portraying Christ as a modern day person, teaching a modern day approach to solving today's problems. He also served as a Deacon in the church. He helped raise funds for the new kitchen/sleep wing in the Family Activities section of the church to feed and care for the homeless.

"Almost everyone in town considered Jack Evans to be their personal friend, spiritual advisor and outstanding example of a good citizen. We were truly blessed to have him in our town and in our lives," said Donovan Cox, Personal Assistant to Mr. Evans.

The family requests that donations be made to the Jack Evans Development Fund in care of The First National Bank of Duchess so that his work with young people can continue."

Donovan looked up from where he had been reading. "How does it sound to you?" he asked. "And is there anything you want to add or to change?"

"Actually, I do have one change, Donovan. My name is Merle, not *Merlie*. Please make that one change and then as far as I'm concerned, it's good to go. Will you handle the distribution to all the newspapers and to the people who knew Jack?"

"Of course," said Donovan.

"So if that's all, I have a couple of appointments to go to."

"Anywhere I can drive you? I know that Jack drove you to all of your appointments and I will be glad to do the same, since you don't drive."

"Donovan, I learned to drive at the convent and I have a driver's license, so I certainly am able to drive. Jack just wanted to know everywhere I went and whom I might see, but things are different now. I fully expect to be my own woman, and that includes driving. But thank you for offering, anyway."

And with that, Merle walked toward the front door and opened it. Donovan had no choice but to leave, so he did.

Chapter Seven

The phone calls began shortly after Donovan left. Merle barely had time to think about what she could do with Lucky Charm when Frances called.

"I'm going to the grocery store some time today. Do you need anything?"

"Actually, Frances, I'm going myself later this afternoon but I do need something—"

"Anything I can do to help—"

"Frances, do you like dogs?"

"Love 'em. I used to have a dog, but I had to leave him with my son when I moved here. I sure do miss him."

"Well, I bought a dog...uh, recently, and I need someone to dog-sit for me while I go to the beauty parlor and a few other places. Could I leave him with you at your house for a couple of hours?"

"Of course, honey. Oh, I'm going to enjoy doing this. But Merlie, Oh, I'm sorry *Merle*. I thought you couldn't drive?"

"Jack didn't want me to drive and he liked to know where I was going, so he did all the driving. But I have a license and everything, and I need to get back into the swing of things, and today is as good a day as any to get out."

"Well, that's a good idea. Getting out, I mean. I'll be right over to pick up…what's his name?"

"It's *Lucky Charm*…and he's still just a puppy, but he's so funny and he makes me laugh."

"Just what you need, honey. I'll be right over to get him."

As Merle opened the door to the spare bedroom, Lucky Charm was sitting there, as if expecting her. He lifted his right paw. She shook it solemnly.

"Well, how are you, Mr. Lucky Charm? Guess what? You are going for a play date with Frances and you are going to have F.U.N.! Her doggie can't live with her and so she is going to love on you until I get back."

Merle picked up his toys and got a can of dog food and dropped everything into his little bed, which conveniently folded in the middle. Merle met Frances at the back door, bed in one hand and dog under her other arm.

"He already had breakfast and he eats about 11:00 or so. Just give him a third of a can of his food and a bowl full of water."

Frances was giggling as Lucky Charm licked all over her face, his tail wagging at helicopter speed. "Oh, it's just so good to have a sweet puppy in my arms again. Now, honey, you go on and do whatever it is you are going to do and we will be fine."

Merle thanked Frances and started for her purse when the phone rang again. It was Donovan.

"Merle, I am so sorry to tell you this, but we can't have the reading of the will this afternoon. Your sister-in-law has called me to say that she has a copy of Jack's will that he wrote *after* he and I wrote this one. I am to meet her at the airport later today and we will do all we can to determine which one is valid. Oh, and by the way, she said to tell you to have her bedroom ready because she will be staying with you for a week or ten days until this is all settled. I will call the other people who were to come today and let them know the situation—"

"NO!" Even Merle was surprised at the tone of her voice, how strong she sounded. "Donovan, we will proceed with the reading of the will as planned. You will read the version that you and Jack have legally drawn up."

"But, Dolores and her husband won't even get here until later in the day —"

"That's fine. They could have taken an earlier flight. And Donovan, please call the hotel and make a ten-day reservation for Jack's sister. She will NOT be staying here, so I want you to take them to the hotel on the way back from the airport. If there is a fuss, tell her to take it up with me."

There was just the slightest hesitation in Donovan's voice, followed by suppressed laughter. "Yes. Yes, I surely will do just what you asked. So...see you at 2:00 at my office?"

"I'll be there."

Merle grabbed her purse and almost ran out the door. She had a hair appointment to keep.

Merle found out that although Jack had driven her everywhere, she had no trouble getting herself to any place she wanted to go. Right after their honeymoon, Jack had told her that he had "made inquiries" from the women in his office at the bank and they all seemed to think that *The Bobby Pin Salon* would be the best place for her to get her hair done.

Last year, Jack had called and talked with the owner, Lucille le Vale, (whom he had never met) and had decided that Merle should have a standing appointment so that she looked nice for the social events he took her to. There were always photographers present at these events, and Jack had been told that if a lady had her hair well groomed and a nice dress on, she would look great in every picture. So the cost of such a frivolous thing as having someone else wash and dry and cut and curl and comb out Merle's hair made sense in a PR kind of way. Jack explained that he wanted Merle's hairstyle to stay the same, so that she always looked the same. Jack specifically set the appointment times for 1:00 p.m., when the ladies in his office would be at work. That way, they would never see Merle in a beauty shop setting.

Jack also told Merle how important his reputation was in the community and warned her not to talk about him or herself, while at the beauty parlor. She was also forbidden to express any opinions she might be asked about or to comment on anything she might read in the local paper or hear from anyone else, outside of the two of them.

"People who do women's hair will try to gossip with you" he said, "and they will then pass this private talk on to the next person who comes in and before the day is through, everyone will know our business." It was for this reason that he never went into the salon; he let Merle out of the car at the handicapped ramp and told her to just walk on in. He had instructed Lucille to bill his office, so there was nothing for Merle to do but go in, sit down, keep her mouth shut and — one hour later — be picked up by Jack.

But today was different.

The salon looked different somehow. She looked up and saw the sign, *The Bobby Pin Salon* and underneath it, the plaque that said *"Lucille le Vale, Owner and Master Hair Stylist"*. The outside had always looked so respectable, red brick with tall windows framed in white with fancy brickwork arches. It looked like something from Williamsburg, one of the places she and Jack had gone on their honeymoon.

It was when she walked through the salon doors that she saw — and felt — what was different. The whole interior had been remodeled. The gold tones were immediately warming and welcomed her into a walled area of modern art so colorful and exciting she hoped she would have to wait so that she could enjoy just looking at them. The modern chairs looked comfortable and she slowly eased down into one of them.

Almost immediately, the receptionist came forward and asked if she could get Mrs. Evans something to drink or perhaps a cookie? Declining, Merle followed the woman back into the salon where all the stylists were busy washing hair or massaging scalps or, towels wrapped around their heads, some women were watching TV programs or watching a TV stylist walking her audience through the latest hairdo from shampoo to comb-out.

The receptionist took Merle's arm to guide her into Lucille's private space. The chair was elegant as was the mirror in front of it. To one side there was a granite countertop station area with a beautiful cabinet underneath it. Next to that, housed under the countertop in its own space, was the wheeled cart that held all the items one would need to wash, dry, cut, and style hair.

Lucille was a tall woman and she probably was the most colorful person anyone would ever meet. She had voluptuous curves, which the women envied and the men were secretly thankful for. Her hair had many colors embedded in it, but it was mostly reddish brown. Merle noticed that there was even a piece of purple hair tucked in behind Lucille's ear. Her hair was styled in a cute stacked bob, "to show off my wild side."

Merle remembered when she told Frances who her hair stylist was, Frances said, "Oh, everybody likes her. She really cares about people. She's not afraid to try out the newest styles or make up. She knows about fashion and art, and she goes to the museums and galleries around the area. She also loves to eat good food and dance and she and her husband go out whenever they can. She's so upbeat. People tell me that they can talk to her about anything. She's a fun person, but I have to warn you...she's a hugger! She'll hug you and then cheer you up and then give you great advice on how to feel better."

Merle thought about this as Lucille came towards her with outstretched arms, saying, "Oh, honey, I heard about Jack's passing and here you came on anyway to get your hair done. Oh, my Lord, girl! I am so sorry to hear about your trouble. I just want to offer you my heartfelt condolences. Wasn't his death sort of sudden? And he was still a young man, too, wasn't he? So what are you going to do?"

Before Merle could get a word out, Lucille had her in the chair and said, "Now before we wash your hair like I usually do, I want to find out how you're feeling."

After months of NOT talking to Lucille, Merle had a moment of indecision, and then she heard herself begin to talk with the words flowing out, softly but with a great deal of controlled emotion.

"Lucille, I need your help. First it was my name. Jack called me Merlie and so did everyone else, but my name is *Merle*. I like my name. It is the only link I have with my mother, the only thing the orphanage let me keep of hers. Then I bought a puppy and he makes me laugh and I love him! I don't think I ever knew what love was until I held him in my arms and hugged him and danced around." Merle half-rose from the chair and Lucille grabbed her and hugged her again and said, "I bet that your puppy is just the cutest little doggie ever." They hugged again.

"But there's so many things wrong. Jack's sister said she was coming to have *her* copy of Jack's will read later this week, but we were supposed to have the reading of the will this afternoon and I told Donovan to get Dolores a hotel room and that we *were* going ahead with the reading of the will and I'm not smart enough to figure all this out. I need someone to tell me what to do who is more *my* friend and not on Jack's side." Now both of them had tears streaming down their cheeks. Merle sat back down in the chair.

"I'm sure you are feeling bad because of the loss of your husband—"

"No, actually I'm fine with that. I mean, we all have a time to die and his time had just come, so I don't feel bad at all about that. But Lucille, something's wrong, and all Jack's friends know it and his sister knows it, but I don't know what it is and it's making me crazy! And I am so embarrassed to talk to you about my private life and all—"

"Sounds to me like you have a right to be mad. Girl, you've been had, if he was keeping things from you that you should know about. I'd be mad too. So don't you be feeling sorry about letting it all out. Honey, that's the first step towards healing, to let it all out. You just cry as much as you want to."

"Lucille, I have to go to the reading of the will in just under an hour, and look at me. I look like a little girl. Can you do anything to make me look older?"

Lucille started to laugh and the more she laughed, the more Merle started to laugh. As Lucille laughed she started to section off Merle's hair and then put a hairstyles magazine in her hands.

"Most women who come to me want to look younger, but you come in here wanting to look older? That's too funny! But you know what? You *need* a new look to start your new life without Jack. And you need a look that will make people take you seriously, make them know *you* are in charge now, and make you look good in the process. Turn to page 78...you see that hairstyle? I can get you shampooed, cut and dried and styled in that look and that will get you through today. Or maybe you just want to continue with the look you have now?"

"NO!" Merle almost yelled. "I need to look...powerful."

"Well, we are definitely going to get rid of all this frumpy hair style that Jack insisted you have. This will make people sit up and take notice today at your meeting. Then, next week when you come in, we will put together a plan for a complete makeover. Would you like that?"

Merle took a deep breath and thought, "Is this what it is like to have a friend, someone that you can laugh and cry with, someone who knows more than you do and can advise you, but who doesn't want to *control* you?" This feeling that she was experiencing was second only to dancing around the room with Lucky Charm. What a great day this was shaping up to be.

Chapter Eight

Merle barely made it to the building where Jack's office was housed. But she wasn't going to Jack's office; Donovan's office was in a different part of the building. She arrived at his office door right on time. As she opened the door, the receptionist looked up.

"May I help you?"

"Yes. I'm here for the reading of Jack Evans' will."

"Oh, you must be his sister. Please go on in. Almost everyone is here now. Mr. Cox will be there in just a minute. He just got a phone call." And with that, she opened the door for Merle, who walked in and sat down in the back row.

The office was understated, with wood paneling, wood flooring and beautiful but simple leather furniture with wood trim. It was definitely a man's office, she noted. She recognized Tom Watkins, who handled Jack's insurance; Bob Roberts, who was in sales (she couldn't remember just what he sold);

Dan Newsome, Head of Alumni Relations at Duchess State University. Donovan wasn't here and neither were Dolores and her husband. Strange—she expected more people than this, but she guessed Donovan would sort it all out when he got here.

Donovan's desk faced the rows of chairs, much like in a school-room. It reminded Merle of the schoolrooms in the orphanage, so she felt comfortable in that setting. She began to wonder just what Jack had to leave in a will besides the house and two cars and one truck. She didn't think that Jack had much money because he was always telling her to economize, and not to spend money unless she just had to. She bought the house brands of all the canned foods at the grocery store because Jack told her that *a penny saved is a penny earned* and that over time those pennies would add up. To what, she did not know.

Ah, finally Donovan came in. He sat down, shuffled his papers and addressed the group, checking off names on a list he held in his left hand.

"Tom, Bob, Dan, glad to see you all. And is that Dolores in the back there?"

Heads swiveled. Everyone was staring at her.

"Uh, no, Donovan. This is Merle, Jack's wife."

There was an audible gasp from the men. Glasses came out; Tom turned around and stood up, squinting at her. It dawned on her that they had not recognized her.

"Well, Merle, come on down here in the front row," Donovan said.

After she got seated, Donovan handed her some papers and said quietly, "Your hair looks very nice, Merle."

"Thank you. Now what is this?"

"Well, let's all look at these papers. They are some of the bequests that Jack made. I have already mailed the checks to the following institutions that Jack was so proud to be involved with. What I want from you is to see if there are any that should be added or taken away, so please look them over carefully."

Duchess High School – $100,000

St. Paul The Servant Orphanage in Duchess – $100,000

United Methodist Church in Duchess – $100,000

Duchess State University – $100,000

The Jack Evans Development Fund (First National Bank of Duchess) – $100,000

A few minutes of silence ensued, and then Donovan said, "The Jack Evans Development Fund in care of the First National Bank of Duchess just ensures that the challenge that Jack issued to the Duchess High School students would continue, where bright students can be assured of a college education—paid for by this fund—if they apply themselves through the four years of high school."

Still no one said anything.

"Okay. Well, there are some individual bequests to be made, but first, Jack asked me to share some words of wisdom with you from the late Conrad Hilton, who was one of his business idols. Do you know who Conrad Hilton was? He is best known as an original entrepreneur long before that term became popular. He bought and refurbished hotels until his hotel empire made him a worldwide name in the hotel and hospitality industry.

"His personal beliefs guided his business principles and at the reading of Hilton's last will and testament, he had a special section to be shared with the Directors and Trustees of the Conrad N. Hilton Foundation. These thoughts are as fresh and relevant today as they were the year of his death, 1979. Hilton's Foundation awards annual prizes to exemplary organizations that work to end suffering in the world. It also supports programs for the blind and the homeless as well as education initiatives. Jack wanted me to read these beliefs and principles to you, and I have included a written copy as well in your folders."

"There is a natural law, a Divine law, that obliges you and me to relieve the suffering, the distressed and the destitute. Charity is a supreme virtue, and the great channel through which the mercy of God is passed on to mankind. It is the virtue that unites men and inspires their noblest efforts.

"Love one another, for that is the whole law; so our fellow men deserve to be loved and encouraged — never to be abandoned to wander alone in poverty and darkness. The practice of charity will bind us — will bind all men in one great brotherhood.

"As the funds you will expend have come from many places in the world, so let there be no territorial, religious, or color restrictions on your benefactions, but beware of organized, professional charities with high-salaried executives and a heavy ratio of expense.

"Be ever watchful for the opportunity to shelter little children with the umbrella of your charity; be generous to their schools, their hospitals, and their places of worship. For, as they must bear the burdens of our mistakes, so are they in their innocence the repositories of our hopes for the upward progress of humanity. Give aid to their protectors and defenders, the Sisters who devote their love and life's work for the good of mankind, for they appeal especially to me as being deserving of help from the foundation."

When Donovan had finished reading the Hilton document, he said, "And now we come to the moment we all have been waiting for — Jack's bequests to his friends and family and to his wife, Merle. Incidentally, Jack's sister will be flying in later this afternoon, and I will have a private meeting with her."

"Now, to my friends Tom Watkins, Bob Roberts, and Dan Newsome, I give each man a personal handwritten letter and a check for the sum of $100,000."

"To my assistant, associate and attorney Donovan Cox, I give a personal handwritten letter and a check for the sum of $100,000. I also request that he continue to handle the day-to-day details of my Foundation, and to call on people in the community on my behalf should the occasion arise for guidance in the business of the Foundation. For this, he shall receive an additional sum of $100,000 for each year that he holds this position."

"To my only blood relative, my sister Dolores Gordon and her husband Joseph Gordon, I give a personal handwritten letter and a check for $100,000."

"And finally, to my wife Merle Evans, who has been my companion and dedicated servant, I give the following: Our residence and all its furniture and household goods and whatever contents therein (on which there is no outstanding mortgage or monies owed); our two cars and my truck (on which no money is owed); and whatever personal effects she has bought or been given by me during our marriage (free and clear). All legal documentation necessary to carry out these, my specific wishes, has been given to Donovan Cox, who will keep them for my wife's future use. She will also be given the key to my personal bank deposit box."

"She will also be given a personal handwritten letter and a check for $100,000 for her unrestricted use."

And with this, Donovan said to Merle, "Here are Jack's keys to the cars, the truck, the house, the outbuilding, the bank deposit box, and a separate key that looks like an internal house key, possibly to his home office. Did Jack have a vault or fire box in the house?"

"Not that I am aware of, Donovan."

"Oh, well. No matter. I'm sure you can find what door this key opens. If you need any help, I will be glad to come over and do what I can."

"Well, you are all free to go now. Please call on me if I can be of help." And with this, Donovan gave everyone his business card, and ushered them out of the room. All, that is, except Merle.

He shut the door and took her hands. "Merle, if there is anything I can do for you, please call on me night or day. Jack was especially forceful in making sure that you be treated with the utmost respect. He felt like he had protected you from the world since he first met you, and he has loved and respected you ever since."

Donovan squeezed her hands lightly and let them go, and Merle picked up her purse and the folder she had been given.

"This has all been very upsetting, Donovan. I am going to have to think about what I want to do next."

"Of course, Merle."

"Thank you so much," she said as she started to leave. Then—

"Wait. Donovan, what did Dolores say when you told her about the reading of the will and about her being put up in the hotel?"

"I had to text her, so I can't be sure of how she *felt*, but she did agree to be taken to the hotel, so I guess that worked out all right. I'm going out to the airport in about an hour to pick them up."

"Make sure she knows that SHE is to pay for her room and all her expenses while she is here, AND, she is to call me before she comes over to see me about anything. I do not like, nor do I want, 'drop in' company."

Donovan's eyes twinkled again as he reached for the doorknob and opened the door. "Yes, ma'am." he said.

Merle opened the door and found all three of Jack's friends waiting for her.

"Merle, here's my card. Call me if I can help in any way." They each said this all at the same time, and she took the business cards and crammed them into her purse.

"Thank you, but I've got to run," she said. And run she did, down the steps and out to her car. Never had she been so glad to get out of a parking place in her life.

Chapter Nine

Something was bothering Merle, but she couldn't quite figure out what it was. It had to do with numbers, and she couldn't focus on numbers when her mind was on driving. She knew she had to get home to Lucky Charm, to relieve Frances from his care, but this numbers thing was somehow very important and she had to get it resolved first.

As she paused for a red light, she saw a fixit shop. Maybe that was Brian's shop. He would know what to do. She pulled over, parked and went in. The shop appeared to be empty.

"Hello — ?"

Brian appeared through a door behind the counter, wiping his hands with an oily rag.

"Well hey, Mrs. Evans. What's up?"

"We just got through with the reading of Jack's will and I was on my way home and saw your shop — "

"How did it go?"

"I'm not sure. Donovan read the will and stated how much money was going to which institution or person. Oh, wait, that's it! Brian, the bequests given out as checks at Donovan's office totaled *over a million dollars*! I — we — he — Jack never told me he had money, in fact, just the opposite. I had to scrimp and save and justify every penny because he said we had to be careful with our spending."

"Over a million dollars?" Brian whistled.

"Oh, and he gave everyone a handwritten letter or note or something. Donovan gave out the sealed envelopes. Here's mine — " And Merle put her purse down, got out the letter and began to open it.

"Hold on, Merle. Just wait a minute. If Jack gave you a handwritten letter, then whatever it says is probably legal and binding, not to mention personal. You might want to wait until you get home to read this in private?"

"Brian, I'd rather be with someone I trust than be at home alone." And with that, she opened the letter, and read it silently to herself.

"To my dearest Merlie, if you are reading this, then I am dead. I want you to know that you are the only good thing I have ever had in my life. I tried so hard to do good every day of my life, and I sometimes

succeeded, but I go to my Fate now, where the bad things I have done will be judged and punishment meted out. I have influenced others to their downfall as well and I am so ashamed for that. Sundays were my salvation days because I did no wrong on Sunday, the Lord's Day. It was Monday through Saturday where I was overtaken by the Devil and His ways. What is Man in the face of such Evil? Two people in particular introduced me to the Devil himself, and they now will try to damage your soul as mine has been damaged. Beware of those bearing gifts inside of which are the weapons of your destruction.

I have made provision for you to be able to live in luxury if you want to, or to help others if you want to. I know you to be a pure soul, a truly good person, and I often asked God why He gave you to me to protect and to develop and to care for. All the abuse I suffered at the hands of others crippled me for expressing love to you (or anyone else for that matter), but I hope you do find Love, for it is the only thing that can't be bought, and therefore, the only thing that I truly wanted in this life. Thank you for being kind to me and for working with me in this difficult relationship. Having you as my wife is the only thing I am proud of."

Merle looked over the letter again, and then looked at the check. There must be some mistake. Jack had written too many zeroes on her $100,000 check. She showed it to Brian.

"Brian, tell me how much money this check is made out for? I think there are too many zeroes."

"Looks like a million dollars to me, Merle, and look here—he wrote out the amount, "One Million Dollars and No 100s." He handed the check back to her.

"So what are you going to do?"

Merle thought a minute and then said, "I'm going to take this check back to Donovan. He wrote it out—this isn't Jack's signature—and he is the executor of Jack's estate, so he will be able to tell me what it all means. Are you coming to do the yard today?"

"Yes, at the regular time. Is that still okay?"

"Yes. Maybe by then, I will know more about what is going on."

"Well, until then, don't count your chickens before they hatch."

"What does that mean?" Merle had a puzzled look on her face.

"It means that until you have a million dollars in your hands, you don't have a million dollars. You just have a piece of paper that says you have a million dollars. Look, go on and get back to Donovan's office and see what you can find out about the check.

Merle left Brian's shop feeling better about the check and what she should do about it. Surely Jack wouldn't be so mean as to play a trick on her with the check—or would he? He had played tricks on her before, but nothing this big.

And why hadn't she shared the letter with Brian? He might have been able to shed some light on a side of Jack that she had never known. Jack might have been a bad man, or a verbally abusive man or even an insensitive man, but she never had considered him an *evil* man. But then again, how would she know? She thought of the Devil as Evil Incarnate, but she always thought that she would be able to recognize it. What if, as the song said, "he'd have blue eyes and blue jeans"?

She was humming that tune as she ran up the steps to Donovan's office, hoping that he had not yet left to go to the airport to pick up Jack's sister Dolores. She hurried down the carpeted hallway and turned the corner into Donovan's office area. His secretary was not at her desk, so Merle took a seat, ready to wait until Donovan came out. She glanced at the clock and was surprised to see that it was 4:00. She had left Lucky Charm with Frances for six hours.

She heard voices behind Donovan's door, indistinct at first and then louder.

"Why did you give her the keys? We need those keys and she has no idea what they go to." Merle recognized Tom's voice. "I'm going to call and set up a time when I can go over to the house and talk about insurance with her, and maybe she will give me the key to Jack's office so I can come back and go through his computer records."

She heard Bob say, "I've got to get into that international contact list but I don't know how it is stored in Jack's computer or even if he had a special laptop or something."

"Well, what about the new alumni relations list Jack spent all that time laying the groundwork for? He said he gained ten pounds just going to all those alumni functions and sounding out the people he met as to their preference for 'extracurricular' activities. How do I identify those men? I mean, Jack was the talker, not me. What did *he* say? And what did *they* say back? It's not a topic you can just bring up at the after game festivities. What did he call it anyway? I've got to have a name in order to bring this up in the computer." Dan sounded the most stressed of all three men.

They all talked at once and then Donovan said, "Look, once—and I stress ONCE—Jack referred to what we were putting together as THE FRANCHISE. He wanted a model that needed no customizing but that was instantly recognizable for what it was, and that could be promoted electronically overseas as well as down the street. So try that as a keyword when you get into Jack's computer."

"You mean *if* we get into his computer, don't you? Hell, now that you've given the keys to little miss Merlie-with-a-new-hairdo, we can't even get into his house, much less his office, much less his computer."

Donovan's voice rang out, "What kind of fool do you take me for? Of course we have access to anything Jack possessed, including his wife. I had copies made of the keys and here's a set for each of you. Now, it's up to you to get what information you can any way you can, but don't set off any alarm bells.

"Tom, you get with Merle about the insurance situation. Drag it out over several weeks, meeting with her once or twice a week as you and she slowly go over Jack's insurance documents. Get to know her, let her learn to trust you and soon she will be telling you things she doesn't even know she knows."

"Same with you, Bob. Tell Merle you and Jack were working on a new way to serve an international community, and that you were going to have to look through the computer for Jack's notes on the project to date before you can draw up the business plan that you two were working on. You get to know her as well by being charming and nice and listening to her tell you about her life with Jack. And ALL of you can start by calling her *Merle*, and NOT Merlie.

"Dan, you probably have the hardest job of all. Jack was just now comfortable enough with our Internet security system that he felt we could harvest our *local* 'patrons of the arts', so to speak. The trick is that we have to get information that no one could possibly trace back to us, and then we have to be able to use it in a manner that is not identifiable as coming from us. Above all, NO ONE must know that we are the supplier of the product. We do not manufacture the product. Technically, we don't distribute the product because we are not putting anything out there in the ether to be accessed by anyone at any time indefinitely. We supply specific information to our customers only at their stated request. And our product is temporal; it is only up for consumption for a short time and then — *poof!* It is gone."

There was a moment of silence and then Merle heard Donovan say, "I've got to go to the airport to get Jack's sister and her husband. Stay in touch, guys. Oh, and by the way — you can cash your checks whenever you want. There's plenty more where that came from."

There was a pause and then Donovan's office door opened and out came Tom, Bob, Dan and Donovan. Thankfully, by this time Merle had dashed into the ladies room down the hall and had locked herself in one of the stalls.

"Oh, my God! What have I stumbled into? And what has Jack been doing with these men? I have to talk to someone who can interpret what these guys said. Thank you Jesus that I had a notebook and pen and could take it all down in shorthand. Now, if only I could start breathing again, I might be able to pee."

Chapter Ten

Merle drove home as fast as possible and she wasted no time in parking the car in the garage. Brian was cutting the grass in the back yard, and she motioned him to follow her into the house.

"Brian, you will never believe what I just heard." She put her purse on the kitchen chair and sat down at the table, motioning to him to take a seat as well.

"They were all still there, except for Donovan's secretary. Tom, Dan and Bob were in Donovan's office and they were all yelling at Donovan. They were mad that he gave me these keys—to the house, to the cars and the truck, the outbuilding, the bank deposit box and a separate key that Donovan said looked like an internal house key, probably to Jack's office. But Brian—get this. Donovan gave each one of them a duplicate set of my keys." She showed the keys to Brian, picking up each key as she named it. Then she handed them to him.

Brian whistled. "Wow! Wonder why he did that?"

"Oh, I *know* why he did that. When I got over the shock of some other things he said, I got out my grocery notebook and a pen and took it all down in shorthand. Listen to this. Donovan told Tom to get with me about the insurance situation. And he told Bob to get with me about Jack's starting a new international project. Dan was working with Jack on—what did Donovan call it—'harvesting our local patrons of the arts'? That had a lot to do with the new Internet security system.

"I don't know what the product is, but Donovan stressed that 'no one must know that we are the *supplier* of the product. We do not *manufacture* the product. Technically, we don't *distribute* the product because we supply specific information to our customers only at their stated request.' And then Donovan said that 'the product was *temporal*, only up for consumption for a short time and then—*poof*! It is gone.'"

"Everyone talked all at once about how in the world they were going to do this. Donovan told them that Jack referred to all this as THE FRANCHISE. He said Jack wanted a model that was recognizable and could be promoted internationally as well as down the street, and that they should each use THE FRANCHISE as a password to try to get into their sections of Jack's computer files."

"And then, Brian, he said the scariest thing of all. He told them to 'get any information you can, any way you can, from Merle, and from Jack's home office.' He told them to be charming and nice to me and to listen to me and get me to talk with them about Jack's life. They are to get me to trust them and be friends with them. And he said they could make a good start by calling me MERLE and not Merlie!"

Merle was crying now, shoulders shaking, tears falling on her table. "I am just so scared!"

"Where is Donovan now, Merle?"

"He's gone to the airport to pick up Dolores and Gordon and then take them to the hotel. I don't know where he will be after that."

"Okay. So we have a bit of time. Merle, I think the first thing we should do is to change the locks to the house since everyone has a key. You only have three doors and I can do that easily. Next, I will fortify the windows and reset your alarm system. That should get you safely through the night. I think I have everything I need in the van to do that this afternoon.

"Then tomorrow, you should be prepared for each one of Jack's friends—and his sister—to call on you, either in person or to set up an appointment to visit you later on. Accept any calls and make the appointments as soon as you can, one time slot of a couple of hours a day each for Tom, Bob and Dan. They should come on separate days. Let Donovan come and go as he wants, and by all means schedule a time to receive Jack's sister as soon as possible. Otherwise, she will bother you to death, trying to get her message to you."

"And Merle, I am going to take up residence in your garage for a few days if that's okay with you, and see if we can figure out what's going on and just how much danger you are in. Are you okay with that? You will have to trust me on this, knowing that I am completely on your side and that I want no harm to come to you. So tell no one of my involvement in this or of what plans I have shared with you, understand?"

Brian stood up and Merle did, too. She hugged him and took comfort in his strength and the promise of real help. She had absolute faith that he would figure this all out. She stepped back and smiled, eyes brimming. "Does this mean that we are teammates?"

"You bet, young lady."

"I feel more like a Lady in Distress."

"Then I will be your knight in shining armor—wearing an invisibility cloak for now."

They both laughed and then the phone rang. Brian slipped out of the kitchen and Merle picked up her pen and the notebook. It wouldn't hurt to record every word that any one of these men said to her from now on.

Except the phone call was from Frances.

"Merle, I have had the most wonderful day with this little critter, but he is making whiney noises and I think he misses you. I know he's not hungry because I just fed him. May I bring him over now?"

She had forgotten about Lucky Charm. What a bad doggie mama she was. She could hear them coming across the yard, so she ran to the kitchen door and opened it just in time to be run over by a little black ball of fur chasing its tail round and round. He was barking loudly now — YIP! YIP! YIP! — in a higher register, roundly scolding her for her absence. She kept bending over to try to pick him up but he evaded her every time she came close. She and Frances laughed and laughed at the little critter's assault. Frances then said, "Well, I'll leave you two to your reconciliation." and went home.

"You bad boys are all alike." Merle said. "If I can't deal with you directly, I shall have to play the game and trick you into my lair. Ahhhhhh — GOTCHA!"

Later, after getting some treats and a warm bath, along with many, many tummy rubs and behind-the-ear scratchings, Lucky Charm suddenly sat down, front legs straight. He was listening to something Merle could not hear. That made her nervous. Then she heard it too, a faint knocking on her kitchen door. When she looked out the glass window, she saw Brian and immediately let him in. Lucky Charm's tail began wagging furiously, both ears went up and his tongue lolled out the side of his mouth as he panted happily. He definitely liked the man standing in front of him.

Brian absently scratched behind Lucky's ears as he told Merle the things he had done to keep her safe. He asked if he could try to get into Jack's office with her keys, so that if anything were in Jack's computer, Merle and Brian would have seen it first.

Lucky Charm suddenly slumped and dragged himself to his bedroom where he jumped into his special bed. Merle closed the door. "He will sleep through the night," she said to Brian as she handed him Jack's keys and followed him into Jack's office area.

Sure enough, the interior key opened the office, but now what?

Brian said, "Merle, would you mind if I tried to get into Jack's computer? If I can get in, using the password that Donovan suggested, then I can put another password in its place and that ought to mess up the works for a while. We just need to buy a little time so that we can figure out what's going on."

"No problem," said Merle. "I wish I knew how to use a computer. Jack wouldn't let me continue my education, and I feel so dumb, so 'out-of-it'. When I was in the orphanage, I felt competent, and I so enjoyed learning. My Mother Superior was wonderful, so dedicated to education for all of us girls."

"Listen, when this is all over, Merle, I will personally see to it that you go to college and choose a career for yourself and pursue what you want to in Life. You deserve that for putting up with Jack Evans. And I think that's what he wanted for you, too, if he hadn't had to fight all his demons. At least you have a future to plan for, Merle. Jack was a victim of a horrific past, I suspect. Why don't you contact your Mother Superior and get her advice on how to proceed with your education plans, now that money is no object?"

That thought would sustain her through the weeks ahead, giving her hope and a goal, one she knew she could accomplish. Thank God she didn't have a clue as to what the next few days would be like. She would survive it all only in retrospect. Going through it validated her strong belief in Guardian Angels in general, and her Guardian Angel in particular.

Chapter Eleven

Merle took Jack's key to the interior door and turned it in the lock to the office. The door opened. She reached a hand inside and turned on the lights. Directly opposite the door was a desk, flanked on either side by three six-foot-high cabinets lined with bookshelves. The desk and the cabinets were made of hand-polished wood inlaid with mother-of-pearl. Jack had had them made for his office and Merle never saw them after their installation. There was a safe — old-fashioned, dark green and square — with a dial in the center of a turn wheel. It looked more like a movie set piece than a real safe. It sat between the middle cabinets behind Jack's chair.

Jack's chair was made of fine leather, beautifully hand-rubbed so that it appeared to be glowing, catching every beam of light in the room. It was made for comfort, heavily plumped with silhouette stitching, but was also sturdy enough to handle the heaviest of body frames.

The desk itself had three drawers on each side of a center nook where the chair nested. There was a built-in wastebasket inside the nook, angled to catch whatever came its way. Each of the drawers had a keyhole lock above the drawer pull. The desktop itself had more ornate carvings and inlays and was covered with custom cut beveled glass.

If one were seated behind the desk, you could see whoever came in the door. The back of Jack's chair faced a faux window treatment, as there were no windows in the office. It had one of those daylight bulbs installed above the top of the faux window, hidden by the window treatment, which supposedly followed the track of the sun, providing artificial sunlight throughout the day.

Jack's view also included two three-person couches, one on each side of the door, and two beautiful overstuffed chairs facing his desk. This is where he met with Tom, Bob, and Dan. When the four of them talked, it was easy to pull the chair over to one of the couches where they could face each other.

Gorgeous Persian rugs delineated the desk area from the seating area, rich with gold and deep shades of rusty red and black.

Across the bottom half of the bookshelves were cabinet doors, also locked, and this is where Brian went first. The first cabinet he opened housed a laptop and some peripherals. The other cabinets contained CDs and papers, but no files.

Brian put the laptop on the desk and settled in for a long night's head game to try and find out Jack's passwords and to get to the contents of the computer. Then he and Merle would know what game they were in and could plan accordingly.

Merle said, "I'm going to make some coffee. Do you care for some?"

"Yes, thanks."

When Merle came back in a few minutes, bearing the fragrant coffee, Brian said, "How well do you know Jack and his friends, Merle? And Donovan? What are they like? Tell me anything about them you can remember. Passwords are often made up from the bits and pieces of people's lives."

"I honestly can't think of a single thing, Brian."

"Well, then, let's start with Donovan's suggestion — we'll key in THE FRANCHISE," said Brian.

After a few minutes of frustrating key work, Brian asked Merle if she knew of anything that Jack liked a lot, such as fishing, hunting, banking, friends, or church — something he felt strongly about.

"Nothing comes to mind but I do know something that he *feared* a lot — *apples*. He told me he was allergic to apples and that we were never to buy apples or have any food that was prepared with apples." Merle was awfully glad that Brian couldn't see her face, because it felt hot, and she was sure it was beet red. She had never told anyone about Jack's allergy to apples.

"Well, let's just try that one. Maybe if I add 123 at the end. YEP. We're in. Okay now, that was the gateway password, and how do we get in these doors?"

Brian was looking at a screen that had six rectangles on end, in a row, that looked like six doors. Underneath each rectangle was a place to write in a password. Brian was fully engrossed in trying to think of passwords for the doors based on a person's choices without fully knowing the habits of that person.

"Maybe this is where THE FRANCHISE will work. Yes."

On the screen, the password caused something to be done with the doors. Each one of the doors was outlined in a different colored light and each was pulsating in sequence. It had a gambling casino feel to it.

"Quick, Merle. At the reading of the will, what charities did Donovan name as the recipients of Jack's money?"

"Well, there was the high school in Duchess, and St. Paul the Servant Orphanage in Duchess, and Duchess State University, and the Jack Evans Development Fund—oh, and that's tied into the Duchess High School where Jack challenged the students to make good grades and he would pay for their college educations. And that fund is administered by Donovan, who gets an extra $100,000 a year as administrator."

Brian keyed in *Duchess High School* on the first door in the pulsating rectangle in the middle of the door. The door swung open, with named folders set in a mini desktop. Then he keyed in *St. Paul the Servant Orphanage*. Nothing happened. He went to the next door and typed in *Duchess State University* and the door swung open, revealing folders with different names.

"Okay, what about people? What people were named in the will?"

"Jack's best friends—Tom Watkins, Bob Roberts, and Dan Newsome; then Donovan Cox; then his only blood relative, Dolores Gordon and her husband Joseph. And me, of course"

"Okay, I'm beginning to see a pattern here." Brian typed in *Tom Watkins* on the fourth door and another rectangle materialized underneath that name. Brian keyed in *Bob Roberts*. Another rectangle appeared below that. Brian put *Dan Newsome* in the box. When another rectangle appeared, he tried *Donovan Cox*. When all four names were in place, the door opened, with folders lined up ready to be accessed.

The fifth door stood ready to be opened. Brian tried *Family*, since the first four were *Friends*, and the door swung open, revealing two folders inside labeled Dolores and Merle. The sixth door had *CPR* in the outside rectangle, but try as he might, Brian could not open that door. All the doors were open now except those two: *St. Paul The Servant Orphanage* in Duchess, and *CPR*. Brian had a hunch that they might be related, but he didn't know how. Mentally, he corrected himself. He didn't know how — *yet*.

"I'm in every door except the Orphanage and CPR. Any idea why Jack would password-protect those?"

"Jack never did anything with CPR that I know of, so I don't know what that refers to, but the orphanage is where he and his sister were raised since they were very young. I never found out who their parents were or why they were brought to the orphanage or why they weren't raised by some of their other family members."

"Weren't you raised in an orphanage as well, Merle?"

"Yes, but not the same one as theirs. I grew up in the Duquesne orphanage. My mother superior is there, and Jack and Dolores's mother superior was here in Duchess, but she's not the one who came to the funeral." Merle shivered. "That one is relatively new. The one who came to the funeral has been there only six years."

Brian looked up at Merle. "Are you cold? You've had a very chaotic day. Listen, I've just gone through four of the doors, using the password Donovan gave the guys, plus I've done a quick look into each door of the institutions and they all have to do with spreadsheets for future development along with financial suggestions as to how to raise the monies for the institutions, how to invest it, and how to maximize their tax options. There's really nothing unusual here.

"As for the door for Jack's friends, the information in their individual folders seems to be what I would imagine was in their letters. Even though they were all about the same age, Jack was really a mentor to them, a father figure, and his advice and concern for them runs along those lines. There's nothing unusual here, either.

"I have put a new password on the St Paul The Servant Orphanage door and on the CPR door. There's something there but I'm going to have to spend more time on it. Meanwhile, no one can get in them because they don't know the passwords I put on them."

Merle stifled a yawn. "So can I go to bed now? Suddenly, I am so tired…"

"Yes. I am going to go home now and work on this last piece of the puzzle, and you carry out the instructions I gave you earlier in the day, all right?"

"Sure. Get some sleep, Brian. And thanks."

Chapter Twelve

Merle woke to the singing of birds. She stretched, yawned and lay in bed, listening to their songs. So much variety! Such lovely sounds! She felt like she had not a care in the world — until she remembered that this was the day that Jack's friends and probably his sister were coming over to pump her for information.

"I won't let them ruin this day for me. In fact, I have a poem forming in my mind about the lovely bird songs and I am going to go write it down before I forget it."

She scooped up Lucky Charm, who had been sleeping on the rug beside her bed, opened up a can of dog food and put a third of a can of *Cheesy Chicken* in his food dish. She then sat down at the kitchen table and began to write.

DREAM WORLD

Every night I go down into the Dream World.
I go to lay the Cares of the day in one place
And pick up the Hopes for the coming day
And take them back to Earth.
Sometimes,
I go through Stars
And Moonbeams
To get there.
Other times,
I go through
Dense Thickets
And Darkening Woods.
Very Occasionally,
There is Instant Darkness,
Which I liken to Death,
When it comes.
The best part
Is waking up to birdsong,
A phenomenon peculiar
To our Earth.
The birds are on a schedule
As old as Time.
They have a job—a purpose—
And they carry it out
Relentlessly.
Oh, let me know
With Avian Certainty

What my Purpose is,
And let me meet each day with a song!
Someone Out There
May be listening
And may be blessed
By what You have put in my heart.

After feeding Lucky Charm, who seemed to want to sleep the morning away, Merle decided that he should stay with Frances, considering the unpredictable nature of the day ahead. One short phone call later, Lucky Charm was in the arms of his beloved Frances who was wearing pajamas under her house-coat. Fortunately, their garages were close together and either Merle or Frances could get into each other's houses without being seen.

Sure enough, just at that moment the phone rang and there was a muffled knock at the kitchen door.

Picking up the phone, Merle looked out the curtained window of the back door and saw that it was Brian, carrying a small sack. She unlocked the door and let him in as she said "Hello" to the phone.

"Merle? This is Donovan. I'm giving you a head's up on Dolores. She just left my office, mad as a wet hen. She came to my office about an hour ago, and I gave her Jack's check for $100,000 and the letter that he had left for her. She looked at the letter and the check and then reached in her purse and started waving a signed, handwritten will that she claimed Jack had given her some time *after* the date of the will he had me write up for him. She said he had asked her and her husband Joseph to sign it as witnesses. In it, there are no disbursements to any charities or to any people. It all goes to her, according to her version of the story.

"I hated to disappoint her, but I pointed out that it was a template off the Internet with the blanks filled in in ink and signed in ink by Thomas Jackson Evans." Although that was Jack's full name, he never signed his name that way. The will that I read and made disbursements from was dictated to me by Jack in person, and signed by him in my presence and that of several staff members from his office and mine. It definitely will hold up in court should she continue to contest the will, as she has assured me she will do. She reluctantly left the will with me and told me to 'check it out' with all the legal people I knew and that she was on her way to tell you that she owned everything of Jack's and that you would have to find another place to live."

"What? Oh, no. Can she do that? Make me leave my house?"

"No, and if she tries to make you believe that, just tell her that if you feel threatened by her, you will obviously have to call the police. Then DO it. I'm serious. You should never feel unsafe in your own home."

"Thank you, Donovan, for telling me this. I will let you know how it all turns out."

As Merle hung up the phone, the doorbell rang. Opening the door, she said "Hi, Dolores. Joseph. Please come in." And she led the way to the living room. They sat down and Merle wondered what to do next.

"I guess you are wondering why we're here. I just left Donovan's office. He's such a jackass."

"I beg your pardon? What happened?"

"Well, I thought I was doing him a favor by bringing him Jack's will, the *real* will that Jack left with me in case something should happen to him. But noooooo, that Donovan, he claims to have a 'valid' will that Jack made him the executor of and has signed and has witnesses and everything."

Merle looked at Joseph, wondering how such a meek little man could just sit there, knowing the lies his wife was telling. Oddly enough, upon closer scrutiny, Joseph seemed quite comfortable in his own skin, just an observer as events unfolded.

"Well, what can I do?"

"I'll tell you what you can do, young lady. You can get up off your tush and call this Donovan person and tell him that you and I agree that I have Jack's real will and that his services are no longer needed." She sat, hands folded in her lap, looking triumphant.

"I'm afraid I can't do that, Dolores, because I know for a fact that the will Donovan has is legal and binding. If you are unhappy with that, I will be glad to take back the hundred thousand dollar check that Jack wrote and signed for you."

Merle's steady gaze left no doubt that she meant it. Dolores blinked.

"Give back the check? Well, no…of course not. My brother wanted me to have that check and so much more."

"Well, you either accept that Jack's signature on your check is real — and keep the check, or you accept that the signature on the will that you brought to Donovan's office is real, and give back the $100,000 check. Which is it to be, Dolores?"

This last sentence was said in a firmer voice than Merle had ever heard herself say — and it worked.

"No, now that I understand things better, I am going to agree with you. I guess we'll go back to the hotel now? Unless, of course, you want us to stay here in my brother's house?"

"This is *my* house now, Dolores. As are Jack's cars and the truck, and all the things that he specified that I should have, naming them by name and giving me full title to. And I think it best that you stay at your hotel for the duration of your stay. You may stay there for as long as your budget allows. Donovan specifically told the hotel manager that you were responsible for your charges. Now, if you will excuse me, I have some phone calls to make."

Merle stood up and began walking towards the front door. Realizing that they had been dismissed, Dolores and Joseph scrambled off the couch and went through the front door that Merle held open for them.

The second they left, Merle locked the door and hurried to the kitchen.

"I'm so glad you are still here. I thought I would be too intimidated to talk with her but she's really quite, uh—"

"Pathetic? Sad? Ordinary?"

"Yeah, all of those."

Merle got two cups and poured the still-hot coffee in them. Brian opened his sack and took out two muffins—blueberry for him and glorious morning for her—and they began to eat. In silence.

Then Merle said, "Where do we go from here, Brian?"

"Well, I have several things to talk to you about, and they are very serious things. Last night I did some more research into Jack's computer, especially those two 'doors' that we couldn't open—*St. Paul the Servant Orphanage* and *CPR*.

Merle said, "That orphanage is the one that Jack and Dolores lived in. I really don't know how or why they were taken to the orphanage or at what age or anything about it. Jack was very close-mouthed about the whole orphanage situation. Maybe Donovan would know." Merle got up and refilled their cups.

"You know, the only one who might know is Dolores. How would you feel about talking with her again, maybe tomorrow?"

"Do I have to? Is it really necessary?"

Brian looked at her over his coffee cup. "Merle, Jack was involved in something very evil. Right now, I can't go forward with my investigation without your help."

"Your *investigation*?" Merle went very still.

Have you ever been sucker punched by words? That is how Merle felt at that moment. She had regarded Brian as her friend, ever since Jack told her he had hired a "handy man" to take care of all the chores around the house that Jack either didn't want to do or didn't know how to do. She had known Brian for over a year and never had she suspected that he was anything more than what Jack said he was.

"Who are you, Brian? And who is 'we'? I can't even process the idea that Jack was the—what did you say he was?"

"Merle, I am an FBI agent, and we have good reason to believe that Jack and probably his friends, including Donovan, are involved in setting up an international child pornography ring over the Internet. And I need your help in shutting down this ring before it is fully up and running. I need your help in bringing these people to justice. Will you work with me on this?"

"Child pornography, is that dirty pictures that have little children in them?"

Brian drew in a deep breath. "Merle, let me give you a crash course in what we think Jack and his friends are involved in. The simplest definition of child pornography is the exploitation of children being sexually abused and sharing pictures and videos of that abuse by several means, but especially over the Internet. It may, and often does, show and promote sexual abuse of a child in real time, and centers on sex acts involving children and their adult abusers.

"Children of all ages, including infants, are abused in the production of child pornography. There is a trend towards younger victims and greater brutality. Drugs are involved to make the children compliant; that's child abuse as well. To film these acts and upload them to the computers of adults, who pay to view them, is illegal. To access them so that they can be viewed onscreen without actually downloading the images is also illegal.

"Digital cameras and Internet distribution, facilitated by the use of credit cards and the ease of transferring images across national borders, has made it very easy to get this stuff out to their clients without being traced. Prosecution is difficult because multiple international servers are used, sometimes to transmit the images in fragments to evade the law. Hackers can even gain access to legal computers and store pornographic pictures, without the owner's knowledge, until the hackers access them for distribution.

"At any one point in time there are millions of images on the Internet of children being abused and these acts being recorded, with hundreds of new images posted daily. Just this year, we heard of a single offender arrested in the U.K. who possessed 450,000 child pornography images; and a single child pornography site received a million hits in a month. When one attaches a dollar value to these images, the profits for those who create and disseminate these images is astounding.

"This doesn't even begin to address the viewers of child porn who are *pedophiles*. They are particularly obsessive about collecting, organizing, categorizing, and labeling their collection according to age, gender, type of sex act and fantasy. When these pedophiles save these images, it comes to define, fuel and validate their most cherished sexual fantasies. These images tell us what the pedophile wants to do. It literally tells us their sexual *modus operandi*. These collectors see the children involved as objects rather than as people; they also see their own behavior as 'normal'. They think of it as an expression of 'love' for children rather than as abuse.

"Merle, we are pretty sure that Jack is one of the masterminds behind this particular ring. We think Donovan may be involved at the top level as well, probably in distribution, but he's not the other mastermind.

"We think Tom and Dan and Bob are just providers of information that Jack would formulate into plans that Donovan would then put into action. Jack's three friends may not have had a clue as to how their statistics and information were going to be used. We also think that Jack's sister knows something that may help lead us to the real mastermind. But at this point, we don't think she or her husband were actually involved in this scheme.

"We need for you to talk to Jack's sister and see what you can find out about his background that would lead him into such a dark life. He may have been abused himself as a child. Or maybe they both were abused. I know that won't be easy to bring up in polite conversation, but find out what you can. At this point, any new information will help break up this ring."

Merle sat, stunned. She had heard the terms *child abuse, child pornography, kiddie porn, pedophiles,* but she had no idea the extent of the cruelty inflicted on these innocent children. And to think that her husband was not only involved, but may have also had a hand in helping create and run this ring was beyond belief. It literally took her breath away.

Brian looked at her with concern. Merle was obviously working her way through this in her mind, but she lacked the worldliness and the constant stream of media information to dull her senses so that she would not be horrified by the images he was afraid he had put in her mind. He hadn't heard a sound out of her for the last few minutes. It was as if she had stopped breathing.

"Merle? Please say something. Tell me what you are thinking. Did I go too far in telling you these graphic details?" But Merle slumped down on the table and began crying. At least he thought it was crying.

When Brian used to hunt out West on his uncle's ranch, they occasionally would hear coyotes howling, singly and in packs. It was the most terrifying sound he had ever heard.

Merle was howling now, and it made his hair stand on end.

Chapter Thirteen

66 I feel shell-shocked, Brian," Merle said. "Is *Brian* even your real name?"

"Yes. It's my choice when I work undercover as to how I construct my cover — my personality and my background information — so that I can accomplish my mission without attention being unduly focused on me. *Brian* is my real name, but my last name is something different."

Merle was quiet for a moment, staring at a point somewhere over Brian's shoulder. Unexpectedly, she began talking in a calm manner, as if she had been asked a question.

"You know, I like to look up people's names and see what their name means. The name Brian means Strong, Brave, and Virtuous. Did you know that? That's why I have always trusted you, because I could sense these strengths in you, in the way you conduct yourself around me and especially in your work ethic. Even Jack commented on how well you did your work, and he rarely complimented anyone."

The doorbell rang. Merle looked at Brian, who rose from the table and exited out the back door. Opening the front door, Merle was astonished to see Dolores, this time without Joseph.

"May I come in?" A very subdued Dolores waited at the door for Merle's answer.

"Of course, Dolores. Come in. What's going on?"

Merle walked past Dolores and sat down at the kitchen table. Dolores followed her into the kitchen and took a chair across from Merle.

"First off, I want to apologize for my actions this afternoon, and to explain a few things to you. That is, if you aren't too busy?"

"No, this is a good time, so what is it that you want to explain?

"I don't know what Jack told you about our lives in the orphanage, but I would bet he hasn't told you anything much. Is that right?" Dolores leaned towards Merle, earnestly, hands folded on the table.

"I never understood *how* we got to the orphanage in the first place, but Jack was years older than me, and I don't know if he knew *why* we were sent to an orphanage. Did he ever tell you?"

Merle felt her heart contract painfully in her chest, as the face of an earnest child stared into her eyes. "I'm so sorry to tell you that we never discussed Jack's life prior to the time he began visiting me at the orphanage in Duquesne. I knew he was from another orphanage, St. Paul The Servant Orphanage for Boys and Girls here in Duchess."

Dolores started to tremble and tried to speak, but nothing came out of her mouth. She reached out a hand toward Merle, half rose to her feet, and froze in place.

"Dolores? What's wrong?

Merle put her arms around Dolores as she dissolved into sobs. After her anguish subsided, she turned stricken eyes to Merle.

"Have you ever met anyone who was Evil personified? Who had no redeeming qualities? Who caused pain and suffering everywhere they went? Well, Jack and I lived in a situation like that from the time we were brought to the orphanage until we were no longer wards of the state.

"When Jack turned eighteen, he was put out into society and, with minimal guidance, was told to find a job and a place to live, and then Jack took me to live with him. I did all his housework and functioned as hostess while he began educating himself and moving up the social ladder. Every little bit of money he got, he invested. And he was really good at it. He made money hand over fist. And then he began to give it all away to charities."

"Sorry." Dolores' eyes seemed to have trouble focusing as she struggled to bring Merle into view.

"What was I saying?

"You were telling me how good Jack was at investing."

"Oh, right. So, he bought me a little house and furnished it and then I got a job and met Joseph and got married. And Jack still helps out, even now. He always takes my calls and he treats me like a real lady. We don't fuss or argue like some brothers and sisters. We just don't have any parents to turn to or argue with or talk about."

Dolores stood up awkwardly as if her joints were stiff. Slowly she began to move — herky-jerky — towards the kitchen sink. She turned on the warm water and then began to wash her hands, over and over again. Finally, she turned off the water and, taking a hand towel back to the table, sat down.

"I'm sorry. I feel so dirty talking about that time in my life. Every day I have to take a tub bath or a shower, but it doesn't really help. You see, the stain is in my soul and I can't get it out, can't get clean enough…"

Dolores stood up and started frantically making itching motions up and down her arms, although her nails didn't scrape her skin, just barely touched it. Then she started pinching and pulling at her arms with her hands, right hand to left arm and left hand to right arm, as if pulling off a sweater that was stuck to her arms. In frustration, she raised her arms above her head and shook her hands, as if in some strange primitive dance. These movements climaxed in guttural sounds like an animal in distress.

Then suddenly, she sat down and breathed a sigh of relief. Whatever had held her in its grip was gone. Everything was back to normal — so to speak.

Merle had observed all this behavior from her seated position at the table. She didn't know what to make of it other than to know that whatever caused it came from a very dark place. She reached out her hand to Dolores.

"Dolores, please, tell me what happened. I want to help, if I can."

And Dolores did. It was as if she had been waiting for someone — anyone — to say "What's wrong?" and "How can I help?"

The next hour was a nightmare for Merle, but a catharsis for Dolores. Alternating tears with a downpour of words, Dolores told how both she and Jack had been systematically abused — sexually, physically and emotionally — by priests and nuns in the orphanage in Duchess. Somehow they endured the horror of it because they had each other. Dolores and Jack were able to carve out a somewhat normal existence after they left the orphanage, but they had been warned when they left that they could be returned to the orphanage by the "Death Squad" should they ever talk to anyone about what abuses they suffered there.

Today was the first time that Dolores had ever spoken of her pain, even to Jack. It was just accepted that because they had been at the same facility, they both had suffered the same crimes against nature.

"When I heard from Jack that you were from an orphanage, too, I cried so hard. I wanted to come here and talk with you and tell you that I understood what you had gone through, but Jack told me to stay away. He said you were good and pure and that your main problem was a lack of anything meaningful to do with your life, that—and boredom—but that he was working toward giving you some opportunities that he thought would help. He mentioned the local university and said that you might want to take some courses. I don't know. We really didn't discuss it."

"But Dolores. I had a wonderful experience living at the orphanage in Duquesne. Our Mother Superior took a special interest in each of us girls and had mapped out a plan for us to advance by taking college courses. She said we would find out exactly what we wanted to do by trying out many different things, and she took us on field trips and taught us how to act in public. We were trained to be homemakers, to cook and keep house. We learned to drive and to buy groceries and to keep a budget. We learned the fundamentals of how to raise children (but very little sex education!), and we even learned foreign languages. We learned how to debate, how to get our points across without attacking our debate partners. Oh, how I wish I could talk to Sister Mary Angeline about what I need to learn now, but I don't know how to reach her. I think she is now the Mother Superior to an orphanage somewhere up North. Would it help if you talked to your Mother Superior?"

Dolores went into panic mode again, this time shaking from head to toe. "Not likely, Merle. She was the one who arranged the abuse!"

Chapter Fourteen

"Oh, you can't be serious, Dolores. What nun would participate in something like that?"

"All I know is what happened to me and Jack. He was able to leave the orphanage when he was eighteen. I had to stay there until I was eighteen, a few years later, and could go live with Jack. Until we got out of the orphanage, we thought it was normal and even God's will to do what we were told to do. Then Jack found out while he was in college that a lot of the things we were taught were not true. And when he told me the truth, I rebelled against doing what the nuns told me because knowing I would get out in a few years gave me the courage to resist."

"But Dolores — what did they want you to do?"

Bleak eyes looked at Merle.

"I'm too ashamed to tell you. But it had to do with what I now know is false and wrong. Sometimes we were punished for no reason at all. The ones who could endure it the best soon found out that the nuns knew our weak points and would use that knowledge to maximize the hurt. One of my friends, who was not a true orphan, was living at the orphanage because her father had died and her mother had to work. She went home on weekends. Our Mother Superior pretended to be friendly with her mother and found out all the things this girl was afraid of, or liked, or hated, and she customized her punishment accordingly. And when the girl tried to 'tell on her', the nun told her that there was a "Death Squad" that would swoop down and get her and kill all the people she loved if she told on the nun. Another friend had a little dog...Cujo... and that friend's mother told the nun that she couldn't take care of her daughter's dog any more so she had found a nice home for it."

Merle waited, but Dolores was staring into space, seeing something terrible that Merle couldn't see.

"What happened?"

"The nun told my friend that her mother had picked up her little dog and had thrown it in the fireplace and watched it burn. She said every time it yapped from the pain, the mother would hit it with the fireplace poker and laugh. And when it was finally dead, the nun said 'that's what happens when little girls don't mind their elders. And if you ask your mother about where Cujo is, well then, I wonder what punishment God has in store for you and your friends? '"

The women sat, transfixed at the horror of it all. They both jumped when the phone rang.

"Yes, this is Merle. Yes, I did call to ask Mother Superior Mary Angeline if she could come to my house at her convenience. Well, yes, I'm home today, and I just have a few things to ask her. Thank you for arranging this."

"Dolores, I called our local orphanage and asked where my Mother Superior, Sister Mary Angeline, was and that call was from the orphanage I was raised in. They said she is here in town visiting at the local orphanage and could come over to talk with me in person. I know you will like her, and I can assure you she is not at all like your Mother Superior — what was her name?"

Still caught up in the moment of sharing her terrible treatment and that of her friends back at her orphanage, Dolores barely heard what Merle was saying, but she nodded her head and said "Sister Mary Delmas."

"That's odd, Dolores, the name *Delmas* literally means "*He* who lives in an isolated house." It's not a female name. Nuns usually chose their names with Mary as one half of it and the other name could be that of another nun, or a historic nun, or a family member, even. But I've never heard of a Sister Mary Delmas."

Dolores said, "Well, we often wondered if 'she' was a 'he' because she was so strident and angry all the time, and liked to hit and punish. I can't remember a kind act she did or a kind word she ever uttered. And she was big, too, taller than some of the priests, and heavyset. Come to think of it, she even walked like a man, shoulders hunched over and sort of lumbering when she walked. She was so intimidating. Oh, I can't bear to talk about it!"

The tears came again. It was going to be a long afternoon. But Merle didn't mind. She was learning so much about why Jack was like he was. Maybe if she and Dolores had talked sooner, she and Jack could have had a happier life. She had read that most children who are sexually molested, physically abused, and mentally tormented for a period of time will never lead "normal" lives. There's no magic pill to take to ease the horrendous pain. Nothing turns it off.

And therapy can only aid in helping the person utilize his or her inner strengths to be in control of their lives. To receive the optimum benefits of therapy, one must first identify and acknowledge that bad things have happened; that bad people did them; that these things were not their fault; that it is in the past now and cannot hurt them in the same way, since they now live in the present. Sister Mary Delmas, by telling Dolores' friend that the "Death Squad" would hurt those she loved if she ever asked about her dog, sealed her friend's fate for never being able to acknowledge and thus deal with these childhood problems and people.

The worst abuse to some children can be the unexpected acts of others that trigger emotional responses. For Dolores's friend, hearing a little dog start yapping might forever trigger the horrible mental pictures of a helpless little dog burning in the fireplace as an evil authority figure laughs maniacally while clutching a fireplace poker. And how can you trust a parent who may do these same things to you—and *enjoy* it?

These thoughts were swirling around in Merle's head. How did young children ever sort out *feelings* from *real events* when they were running on fear? And living in constant fear without someone to lean on, to tell them the truth, to love them unconditionally is destructive as well. It means you aren't going to be able to turn off your mind enough to get a good night's sleep, much less be able to function properly in a world whose inhabitants have not shared these experiences and therefore have no idea of the depth of your fears.

Flashbacks are the hand grenades of the mind to an abused person, and no one can predict when one or more will be lobbed at you when you are in the presence of your enemies or even your friends who could unknowingly trigger a painful memory that would result in an unorthodox reaction.

Merle was beginning to understand the dichotomy that Jack lived with, his dual nature, so to speak. He wanted to *be* good, and so he tried to *do* good. But in fact, he was damaged goods and that had been rammed down his throat every day of his early life in the orphanage. Not ever having experienced love

as a child or as an adult, he had to teach himself *how* to love —
like a brother to Dolores; like a protector to Merle; like a friend
to Dan, Tom and Bob; and like a father figure and mentor to
Donovan. Suddenly, she felt a surge of pride that Jack, her Jack,
had done a lot of good for a lot of people. All the scholarships;
all the money given to education and the church; all the time
and help he had given to untold numbers of people — without
thought of recompense or recognition.

Of course, this was just the moment that the phone rang.
It was Tom.

"Merle. Listen, I'd like to get started on this insurance program
that Jack mapped out for you as soon as possible. Could I come
over in an hour or so to just ask a few questions, you being an
orphan and all? I don't get many orphans and I am probably
going to have to put this together in a little different way from
what I am used to doing — "

"Hi, Tom. Thanks for your call. My Mother Superior is coming
within the hour and I am going to introduce her to Dolores,
who is here now. Why don't you come over about 4:00?"

"Great. I'll see you then."

No sooner had he hung up than the phone rang again. It was
Bob, asking the same question. Merle took a wild guess and
said, "Does Dan happen to there with you? And if he wants to

come too, and get started on all the questions that I know all three of you men have, then why don't you all come at 4:00?"

Just on a hunch, Merle dialed Brian's number.

"Hey. Well, I've got a Mother Superior and three BFFs coming over this afternoon. Are you interested in being present in some form or other? You know, in the flesh or in the ether, that is, electronically?"

"Merle, I will definitely be there in person. Soon I will be able to tell you everything I have learned just today about this case, but not now. Let me know if anyone else calls or comes over."

Dolores had opened her purse and had taken out a compact to repair the damage caused by all the crying she had done. But it was useless. Mascara had run down her cheeks, making her look like a very unhappy clown. She turned her face to Merle.

"Have you got any home remedies for this?" She pointed to her face. Merle started to giggle. Soon Dolores was giggling, too, and then they both dissolved in helpless laughter, which led to coughing and then to burps and other silly noises as the fits of laughter subsided.

"Well, that felt good," said Dolores, taking a deep breath.

"It helped me, too," said Merle. "But I don't think any home remedy will help either one of us in the make-up department.

Let's wash our faces and then seek professional help. And I know just who to call." And with that, Merle dialed the number for *The Bobby Pin Salon* and made an appointment for her and Dolores at 6:00 with Lucille.

And then, the doorbell rang. Merle opened the door and said, "Yes?" And a deep voice asked, "Are you Merle Evans?" Merle nodded just as she heard Dolores scream.

"What's the matter, Dolores?"

"It's HER! IT'S HER!! It's the "Death Squad" coming to kill me!"

And with that, Dolores started running through the public rooms of the house, like a cornered animal looking for a place to hide. She was a child again, a very terrified child. And she would run in circles until she found a way out, even if it killed her.

Chapter Fifteen

It was unnerving, to say the least, to hear a grown person yelling and to see her running erratically, crying hysterically and making unhuman noises.

Merle, fearing that Dolores had had some kind of flashback, began closing the door on the visitor.

"I'm so sorry. My sister-in-law is not well and I need to take care of her. Would you please leave now and come back in— say, half an hour?" She shut the door and locked it, noting the time. It was ten of four now, and there would be time enough to deal with Jack's three friends when they came at 4:00.

Merle took a deep breath and said "Dolores?" She did not see her in the open area that comprised the living room, dining room, and formal entryway.

She went down the hall to the bedrooms. She thought she heard voices from the guest bedroom. That was Lucky Charm's bedroom. Had he learned to talk, now?

"Dolores?" The door opened and there stood Dolores with Lucky Charm in her arms. He was licking her chin and her cheeks and her ear lobes, and Dolores was just beaming. Nothing like Dog Therapy to make you feel good again. Unconditional love happens at all hours of the night or day, and works especially well in emergencies — which this day had plenty of — and more coming, apparently.

Merle scratched under Lucky Charm's left ear. "Lucky Charm! Are you trying to eat Auntie Dolores up? Are you giving her shugs and kisses? Or maybe you're hungry? Do you want some *foods*?" He understood Merle's high-pitched dog patter and began panting and drooling to let her know it.

Upon hearing the keyword — *foods* — Lucky Charm wiggled out of Dolores' arms and leaped into Merle's arms. The two women walked toward the kitchen, talking baby talk to Lucky Charm, who didn't seem to mind as long as they all wound up in the kitchen where the food was.

Merle quickly opened the refrigerator and, taking a can of "Mom's Chicken Pot Pie" from Lucky Charm's shelf, she scooped out a third of a can and put it in his dish. She then set the dish down on the floor in the laundry room, where his water was. There was a dog bed beside a rocking chair in front of the tall window that overlooked the woods at the end of the backyard. The view was serene and peaceful, with the leaves a blaze of autumn color. Dolores sat down and watched Lucky Charm wolf down his food.

"He'll be happy in here and we won't have to deal with him until all this is over," Merle said. "Would you please stay with him until these self-invited guests come and go? And then you and I can go to *The Bobby Pin Salon* and see Lucille."

"Until what's over, Merle?" But Merle had already closed the door and headed back to the living room.

The doorbell rang and Merle opened the front door. "Come in, Tom and Dan and Bob. All three of you together, just like old times when you guys met Jack here to go fishing or hunting or whatever it was you did together."

The men looked at her, stunned. Was she making fun of their good times with Jack?

"So sorry, guys. I guess that sounded a bit callous, but seeing the three of you together just brought back such good memories, especially of Jack. Now, come on in and sit down and let's see what kind of information you need from me."

At that moment, Brian knocked at the back door and Merle stood up. It was a very different looking Brian who let himself in to her kitchen area and walked into the living room. This was Brian Malley, FBI field agent, and he had on the official raid jacket and hat that had **FBI** emblazoned on them so as to be clearly identifiable. There were three other agents with him; all dressed alike—and all armed.

Each agent went to one of Jack's friends, and handcuffed him as they quietly stated the Miranda Rights warning. *"You have the right to remain silent. Anything you say can and will be used against you in a court of law. You have the right to an attorney. If you cannot afford an attorney, one will be provided for you. Do you understand the rights I have just read to you?"*

In the twenty seconds that it took to read these rights, the FBI agents had walked their charges out the back door and into sleek black cars which would take them to the FBI field office downtown, leaving Brian behind. Quick and quiet, just the way Brian wished all arrests could be made.

It was then that Brian told Merle the details of the FBI investigation of the activities that Jack was involved in. The last business meeting that Jack had with his friends was in Donovan's office and Jack had specifically given each one of them assignments to look into and report back to him and Donovan so that their new business venture — THE FRANCHISE — could go forward.

Today, Jack's friends had been charged with criminal acts using computers to commit fraud, both domestically and internationally. Earlier, the arresting agents had gone to the offices of each of Jack's friends and had confiscated their computers and other items of interest to be checked more thoroughly back at the FBI field office. Further charges were possible; and current charges could conceivably be modified or dropped altogether.

Brian told Merle that the FBI was investigating Jack's friends to determine or rule out the extent of their possible involvement in Jack's criminal activities.

Merle said, "What kind of criminal activities are you talking about?"

Just as Brian began to answer her, the phone rang. It was Donovan.

Merle put her hand over the phone and said, "Brian, it is Donovan. Should I take this call?"

"Oh, yes — by all means take his call." Brian took the phone out of Merle's hand, pressed OK to unlock it and put the phone on speaker.

"Merle. This is Donovan. I've been trying to get in touch with the guys. I understood they were coming to your place this afternoon. Have you seen them?

"As a matter of fact, I have seen them. They just left, in handcuffs, with the FBI."

"What the holy hell is going on at your place? Did you say that the FBI was at your house and that they were all arrested, handcuffed and taken away? Is this some kind of sick prank?"

Before Merle could say a word, Donovan started yelling into the phone. "Now the FBI is here in *my* office! What have you said or done to bring this down on us, Merle?"

Brian took the phone from Merle and spoke into it. "Donovan, this is FBI field agent Brian Malley. We have arrested you and Jack's friends under the FBI's Innocent Images National Initiative. This has nothing to do with Merle, who is an innocent bystander in these events, but it has everything to do with you in particular.

"Formal charges will be filed this afternoon, to determine where you fit into the areas of online organizations, enterprises, and communities that exploit children for profit and/or personal gain; major distributors of child pornography, such as those who appear to have transmitted large volumes of child pornography on several occasions to several people; those who produce child pornography; individuals who travel, or indicate a willingness to travel, for the purpose of engaging in sexual activity with a minor; and large volume possessors of child pornography."

Then Brian snapped the phone shut and handed it back to Merle.

"Well, that may be the last time you hear from Donovan, Merle. But if you do hear from him, be sure to let me know by calling my cell. Where is your sister-in-law, Dolores?"

"Come this way, Brian. She's much happier now than when you last heard from her." Merle opened the door to the laundry room where Dolores was still enjoying the view from the rocking chair. Dolores put her finger to her lips, indicating that Lucky Charm was asleep in his dog bed — snoring loudly and occasionally moving his legs as if running in his sleep, barking and whining. Trying to contain her laughter, Dolores stepped into the hall and quietly closed the door.

"He's so funny." Dolores said. But seeing the serious looks on Merle and Brian's faces, she said "Uh-oh. What's up? And why do you have that FBI outfit on?"

Brian spoke first. "I work for the FBI, Dolores, and we need your help. In a few minutes, one and maybe two nuns will come here to see Merle. One of them is Sister Mary Angeline, who was Merle's Mother Superior at the orphanage where she was raised. The other one may be Sister Mary Delmas, the Mother Superior at the orphanage where you and Jack were raised."

Brian stopped as Dolores began to hyperventilate. He had a stern look on his face as he spoke.

"Dolores! Man up! You have a chance to take this woman down today with your witness and your testimony. All you have to do is get her to talk to you about your experiences with her, and Jack's experiences that he told you about. Think of all the children she has crippled — mentally, physically, spiritually and emotionally—by her constant, inhumane behavior. She has lied to you, over and over. But the worst lie was the story she made up about the "Death Squad" so that you would never be able to seek help for the hurt she inflicted on you. She has damaged your ability to trust other people, to love other people, and to build relationships with other people.

"You couldn't handle this monster as a helpless little child. But God has given you an opportunity today to bring down this monster. You may not think that there is a weapon big enough to bring her down, but I am here to tell you that when good people stand up to evil, God and His angels are among them, and good will prevail!"

Dolores stopped shaking and stood straighter, shoulders back, head up, butt tucked in. A light began to shine in her eyes that had not been there before. She listened intently to what Brian was telling her. In effect, he was giving her marching orders for the battle that was only moments away.

"Now, when Sister Mary Delmas comes in, Dolores, I want you to think of David and Goliath. You may feel as small as David, facing someone as large as Goliath. But the best defense is a good offense. Catch her off guard. Start your attack by telling Merle all the things that you and Jack suffered at her hands and if she denies or argues, pick up the stones of truth, fit them into your slingshot, and fire away!

"Tell everything you know — or that you have heard or suspected — about this vile person. I will be back here in the kitchen, ready to protect you if she tries to harm you. There are other FBI agents who are coming here as we speak, who will arrest her and take her away. She will never bother you again."

The doorbell rang, and Brian stepped back into the kitchen area, behind the pantry doors, hidden from view. Dolores went with him, ready to do battle when Brian sent her into the battlefield. Merle went to the door and opened it.

"Hello. I am Sister Mary Delmas, former Mother Superior at St. Paul the Servant Orphanage.

"What is it that you want, Sister?" Merle sat down on the couch and indicated that Sister Mary Delmas should sit on the adjoining couch.

"Well, you see, I need to ask you some questions about Jack. You and he had been married for how many years?"

"We had a five-year-anniversary celebration a couple of months ago. May I get you some coffee? Tea? Perhaps a soft drink? Water?"

"No, thanks. Jack told me that he had some information for me on a thumb drive. It probably has something on it identifying it as belonging to me."

"No, I'm sure I would have noticed that and put it up in a special place for you. We've been cleaning out Jack's office and boxing up his belongings. Some of his computer files we haven't been able to get in to because they are password-protected and we don't know what the passwords are, but we are having a computer expert come in tomorrow mid-morning to work with the files until they give up their information. But no, nothing obvious so far."

Abruptly, Sister Mary Delmas stood up. "Oh, dear. Look at the time. I really must be going. May I come back tomorrow afternoon to see what progress your computer experts have made?"

Merle had risen when Sister Mary Delmas stood up. She walked toward the front door and opened it. "Of course. I understand. Please do count on coming back tomorrow and together we will look the office over with a fine-tooth comb, and I'm sure we will find what you are looking for."

Sister Mary Delmas walked out the front door and got into her black limousine, speaking loudly to the driver, telling him to hurry back to the orphanage.

Merle watched behind the glass door. Brian came up behind her. Dolores peeked around the kitchen pantry doors and said, "Is she gone?"

"Yes, she's gone, but she will be back tonight—isn't that what you meant for her to do, Merle?"

Brian was almost laughing when he made this accusation to Merle.

"I don't know what got in to me, Brian. All of a sudden, I just thought she deserved more grief than I could afford her in the living room alone, so I hope she took the bait I laid out, and will come back tonight and try to jimmy the lock open."

"I can pretty much guarantee that she will at least try, Merle — and then I will be able to say something I have wanted to say all my life, '*Smile! You're On Candid Camera!!!*'"

Chapter Sixteen

Agreeing to meet later that evening at Merle's house, Brian left. Merle and Dolores gathered their purses and left for *The Bobby Pin Salon*, knowing that Lucky Charm would sleep for several hours. Warm bed, full tummy, empty bladder—these all add up to a nice long nap for young'uns, human or canine.

At the beauty shop, Lucille was waiting for them. She had an assistant wash their hair while she finished her last client, and then came in to talk with both of them as they sat in front of her long mirror, looking like skinned rats.

"All right, ladies. What do y'all want done? A style cut, for sure, and maybe some highlights? A totally different color? Are we going to get funky? Be stylish? What image are you trying to project, Merle?"

"Well, I'm thinking about going to college. What do you think about that?"

"Honey! That's great! My grandmother used to say that a good education is something that no one can take away from you. So what are you going to study?" As she was talking, Lucille was running her fingers through Merle's hair, pulling it this way and that, to see what various styles would look like.

"Well, I am going to talk to my Mother Superior about that, but she used to say that I had a knack for working with people. She said I was better behind the scenes than in front of people, but I think that was because I always felt invisible."

"You! Invisible? What are you talking about? Look here, look in the mirror. Now young lady, you look at those soft eyes and those full lips. Why, people go under the knife for lips like yours. And by the way, what was the reaction to your haircut last week?"

"Well, Donovan didn't recognize me. He thought I was Jack's sister, Dolores. He did tell me later that he liked my hair." Merle giggled, remembering. "The secretary didn't recognize me, either, and I've been to Donovan's office several times."

"And what did they say when they realized it was you?"

"Donovan said my hair looked very nice, and the other men were smiling, so I guess I didn't look too bad."

"Well, that man wouldn't know a great hair style if it bit him in the butt. But we don't care. We are giving you a hair style that will attract the young, handsome men you are going to meet in college." Lucille then told Merle that this haircut could be styled in several different ways.

"Now, for your college look, you will need to wear your hair a little straighter than today. So I'm going to not volumize it so much, just put a little product in this time. And your makeup should be downplayed a bit. Use a minimal amount of eyeliner and mascara. Sort of like these." And Lucille pulled out a drawer full of eyeliner and mascara products, and eye shadows and all kinds of make up. Merle was dazzled! Never had she seen so many options in such a small space.

Lucille motioned for Dolores to roll her chair on over to the left of Merle, and she began taking out products, looking at them and choosing or putting them back. "Let's see, now...I think earth tones will work best for you, Merle. They will complement your hair and skin color best for your college look. And you should wear just a touch of eyeliner and mascara. You are going for the natural look here, to just enhance your natural beauty. The key thing to remember is that with you, *Less is More.*

"However, when you have important meetings, where you have to be strong or to get your point across among people you think are better than you, don't hide your natural assets. Wear your hair like we did it when you went to the reading of Jack's will. That got some attention, didn't it? And your makeup should be bolder browns, bronzes, and golds to show off your serious side, just the kind of attention you want.

"Remember when you told me that you look like a little kid to yourself? Bold color will make you look more mature, but not older. It is a confidence builder. You need the color, so if you don't wear color everywhere—your hair, your make up, your clothes—you will look washed out, and you will give the impression that you don't care enough to let people know who you are."

All this time Lucille had been fiddling with the products, trying first one color and then another, until she had the effect she wanted. She had combed and dried and styled and smoothed Merle's hair until it shone. The total effect was stunning! Merle could hardly believe her transformation. Lucille gave her a hand mirror so that she could see the back and sides of her new look.

"Well, what do you think?"

Merle's face glowed in Lucille's mirror like when she looked at herself holding Lucky Charm for the first time. This was a great new look.

And she liked what she saw.

"Now, young lady, we are going to work on your friend's hair, and then, if you have time, we are going to talk a little bit more about what to wear. And I know you gals are rich, but even the rich people I know love a bargain, so I am going to tell you how to be beautiful head-to-toe — on a budget."

Dolores had been listening to all this chatter, watching her sister-in-law transform from an *okay* look to a *dynamite* look under Lucille's masterful hands. Lucille pulled Dolores's chair over to the mirror while her assistant moved Merle's chair back where Dolores was, put her hands on her hips and said, "Honey, what took you so long to get to my salon?"

"Well, I live out of town..." Lucille started to laugh at this literal interpretation of her comment, and as usual, Dolores burst into tears.

"Did I say something wrong?" Lucille, concerned, bent over Dolores and put her hand under Dolores' chin.

"I just don't think you can make me look pretty. I'm not young and I'm ugly and Sister Mary Delmas used to tell me that you can't cure *ugly*."

Lucille stood there behind Dolores' chair, mouth open. Dolores grabbed her hand and said, "Promise me, please promise me that you will make me look good. I have never looked pretty in my life. Sister Mary Delmas told me if I ever wore make up, I would look like a slut. And she told me that if I had thoughts of looking better than the angels, that God would strike me down and my shame would last for Eternity."

"Oh, Lord Jesus, help me out here." Lucille was praying underneath her breath now, because she needed help of the Highest kind.

"Dolores! Do you actually think that God wants you to be ugly? God sees your *inner* beauty, girl. And I try to bring that beauty out in the open so that your very image can glorify God, because you are doing the best you can with what God gave you. If you shine and look good, you will attract other people. I mean, Honey — have you ever seen an ugly angel? You need to look at the outer image of people and then take a look inside them and find their inner beauty, and you both will be glorifying God."

Lucille held her breath. Would Dolores see things this way? Or would she feel that she didn't deserve to be beautiful?

Dolores took a deep breath, looked at her wet-rat image in the mirror and said, "Well, good luck, Lucille. And if it works, I'm going to need a handful of your business cards to give to my friends."

They all laughed, and then Lucille said, "But Dolores, you don't even live here."

They all sobered up. Then Dolores grinned.

"That doesn't matter. I'm going to be visiting my new friend, Merle, at least once a week and now I can afford to fly AND pay for a miracle hair style, too!"

Chapter Seventeen

Lucille picked up several long locks of Dolores' hair, pulling them through her fingers to gauge the health of her hair.

"Honey girl, you are one stressed out child. Your hair is all frizzy and mousy, which shows that you are high-strung and nervous, right? The more stressed out you are on the inside, the more stressed out your hair is going to look on the outside. Lor-dy, Honey! You have got some serious stuff going on inside of you! I know you don't have any man problems because Merle told me you are married to a really nice person. So it's not him. Now, what's going on?"

Lucille was fiddling with Dolores' hair, just as she had done with Merle's hair. Suddenly, she let out a yelp and jumped back. "Oh, my lord!" Horrified, she realized that she had pieces of Dolores's real hair in both hands. Pieces not connected to her scalp.

"Has your hair been falling out? Or have you been pulling out your hair? I noticed you didn't have any eyebrows or eyelashes, but I did not know that you had clumps of hair GONE from your head! What has happened?"

Dolores began to tell Lucille how Sister Mary Delmas used to yank out handfuls of her hair from the time she was a little girl until she left the orphanage to marry Joseph. "She would just walk by me and no matter what I was doing—eating, sitting on the commode, kneeling at the prayer rail, studying—she would tell me that my ugly hair was going to keep me from going to heaven and that she was pulling it out for me while I was little but that I should learn to pull it out, too." This was accompanied by tears and shudders, remembering how much it hurt body and soul.

"Dolores, listen to me! Nothing the Lord has made is ugly. Not your hair, not your toenails, not even the snot in your nose when you have a cold. Your body is a temple and if you treat it right, you will be rewarded with good health. And honey, there is nothing better than good health. I believe all pain comes from mistreating your body. And I think you are in a lot of pain, young lady. You are in need of serious help; help I can't give you, but help I have gotten from others.

"I used to feel like I was just a mess. I didn't enjoy anything. I didn't feel loved. I didn't know how TO love. But I wanted love. And I remember the day I decided I DIDN'T want to keep on living like this. "What were my options? Well, I have never wanted to kill myself. To be honest, I might have felt like I wanted to kill other people at one time in my life, but that's all over. I just love everybody now, some more than others for sure, but LOVE is the main thing in my life. Why do you think I care about you? And Merle? Because some part of me has been where you are now, and since I can't do anything about it but share my experience, then that's the way I will love you.

"When I knew I didn't want my life to be a mess any more, I decided to get some real help. I went to a mental health facility and talked with a counselor and I told him I didn't want to be doped up but that maybe I might try some mild anxiety medication because I couldn't deal with all of this without some help. And I told them I really needed to get all this off my chest and out of my mind. I couldn't deal with it by myself.

"Those people helped me get my life together and taught me how to keep it together. I am a strong woman now, yet sometimes even I break down. But now I know how to get back up and dust myself off without losing it all over the place. I am in control of myself now. They taught me what triggers my outbreaks. And they taught me coping mechanisms, real practical help, step away from the situation or count to ten silently, or speak slowly and quietly to make my point, or breathe in a certain way to get oxygen to my brain. It has helped me to have a life and to run a business. And my husband is so much happier, and it makes me happy because he deserves a better wife.

"But also, you deserve it for *yourself* to feel better, to be in control of yourself. Don't let anybody make you cower in the corner. Some people have waited all their lives to beat you down. They love to watch you in meltdown. You need to show them that you're not going to stay down and that you have come back for real. Remember that song, "I am Woman, Hear me Roar!" Learn the words and sing them when you get down on yourself. There's a fix to everyone's problem. There is always something that can be done to make it better, to ease the pain, to go in another direction, to buy some time. But it won't be smooth sailing. Like the song says, "Sometimes we're the hammer and sometimes we're the nail."

"Send a statement to yourself that this is the *new you*, and that you want to make yourself a happier person, a person who is confident and courageous, and that your life's work now is to make things good for other people, like I do. I just want to make people happy and give them beauty and fun and sunshine and love. That's my gift to give, and you will find your gift, too."

Lucille had been talking non-stop as she carefully combed through Dolores's hair, trying to find the best hairstyle for her. Dolores's natural blonde hair was thick, but it had been neglected and abused for so long that it was dull and lifeless. The bald patches were actually growing new hair because Dolores had not been faithful in pulling the hair out.

"Well, the good news is that this isn't as bad as I thought. So we are going to color your hair a golden blonde with bright blonde highlights. You need some sunshine in your life and this hair color will do it. I will also give you a good conditioning treatment and some shampoo and conditioner to use when you wash your hair back home. Your cut will give you the confidence you need to face that awful woman who seems intent on intimidating you, literally, to death."

Lucille began cutting Dolores's hair and soon it framed her face beautifully. Dolores's eyes popped just from getting her lids out from under the too-long bangs. And an hour or so later, Dolores and Merle sat back in front of the mirror and watched their big reveal.

Both women looked great, Lucille thought. The style and color for each was perfect. But there was no rejoicing, no "YAY", no sound.

Lucille cleared her throat. "Well? What do you think?" She handed each woman a hand mirror so that they each could see her "look" 360 degrees. Still nothing. What was missing?

"Oh, right! You need your make up to truly pull your look together!" And another few minutes were spent customizing each woman's cosmetic tools. First the base coat of moisturizer and make up, just a minimum amount, matched to each woman's skin tone.

For Dolores, who had no eyebrows and no lashes, Lucille penciled in some brows and glued false eyelashes in place. Then came the mascara and eye shadow. Merle had more natural color so she needed only a minimum of eyeliner and earth tones in her make up.

And *THEN* the women squealed like little girls when they saw themselves in the mirror! They came out of their chairs and jumped up and down, holding onto each other's shoulders. Merle was just so happy because she had her POWER look; and Dolores—at last!—was truly PRETTY! They continued to giggle and laugh and look in the mirror and then look at each other and then they got on each side of Lucille and made her jump up and down with them. Lucille kept saying, "Girls, don't cry! Or your mascara will run. Don't Cry!"

Finally, they settled down and paid Lucille and gathered their things to go home, back to Merle's house.

Dolores had told Joseph that she was going to spend the night at Merle's house, sort of a girl's night out. That didn't bother Joseph a bit. What he didn't know was that they were expecting Sister Mary Delmas to take the bait that Merle had laid out for her earlier in the day.

Merle was sure that Sister Mary Delmas would have to go through Jack's computer files tonight before the computer experts came tomorrow, mid-morning. Brian had thought it was a great idea and he had his people in place. He and Merle had "set the scene" for the surprise visit from Sister Mary Delmas, and had talked to Dolores as well to enable her to confront her lifelong worst enemy.

There would be no going to bed this night until it was all over. It was truly going to be a fight between Good and Evil, and Good was going to need a lot of help to prevail!

Chapter Eighteen

It was almost 9:00 p.m. when Merle and Dolores returned from *The Bobby Pin Salon*. Brian came to the back door of the house and knocked. Merle let him in and she, Dolores and Brian went into Jack's office where Brian filled them in on what was happening.

Brian and three of his agents had been in Merle's garage, where Brian had installed his devices. Each room in the house had been set up with microphones and cameras, which could be motion-activated or sound-activated. There was a live feed from the garage to the FBI field office as well. Everything would be recorded in real-time, as it happened, once the front door was opened and the 'visitor' walked in.

"As you know", said Brian, "we are expecting Sister Mary Delmas to try to get into Jack's office later tonight and go through his computer files. She doesn't know that we re-installed the locks to fit the keys that she got from Donovan. That works in our favor because she will be able to enter the office easily and will suspect nothing until she actually gets inside Jack's computer.

"I personally have downloaded everything from Jack's computer, so even if she activates a virus or wipes out the files or websites, we still have everything we need to shut down this operation before it gets started."

"Whoa! Wait just a minute. What do you mean—'Sister Mary Delmas got the keys from Donovan?'" Merle and Dolores asked the same question at almost the same time.

Brian said, "It appears that Donovan is Sister Mary Delmas's nephew. He met Jack when he would visit his aunt at the orphanage.

"We think that the good sister has been working with Donovan for some time now on the project that was being set up to launch in a couple of months, THE FRANCHISE. Jack had asked each of his three buddies to research specific information for a new international business that he was launching before the end of the year. Only five people seem to be involved — Jack, Donovan, Bob, Dan, and Tom.

"We looked into the backgrounds of the three friends and they checked out as being just what they said they were. They were information gatherers. I doubt that either Jack or Donovan wanted to bring these three into a venture that required discretion and loyalty and the possibility that they would more than likely be caught and do jail time.

"Donovan, on the other hand, appeared to have a rather strong connection to Sister Mary Delmas, which was a surprise, considering the fact that he was not an orphan and had never spent time in an orphanage. But the connection with Jack's orphanage made us examine Sister Mary Delmas more thoroughly, and her background is quite interesting. Her brother was Donovan's father, and they frequently visited her at the orphanage. She watched Donovan become an excellent lawyer, one who had a penchant for strategizing, and one who was hungry for money and the things that money could buy. Once Jack came into a power position in the banking industry, Sister Mary Delmas used her connections with Jack to get Donovan the job as Jack's attorney, and much more.

"We found out that there were several other connections that made us suspicious of Sister Mary Delmas, but the real clue came the day I went into Jack's computer, found those doors that Jack had set up and figured out their passwords. What I didn't tell you, Merle, was that I also was able to figure out that the name of the fourth door, CPR, stood for Child Pornography Ring, and *Delmas666* was the password."

Brian had turned on the computer and had pulled up the door in question on the screen.

Both Merle and Dolores stared at the screen with their mouths open, eyes wide, and hearts beating wildly. Both had forgotten how to draw a breath. Suddenly, Merle exhaled sharply and grabbed Brian's arm.

"But Jack didn't know anything about child pornography. Look at all the good things he has done for kids over his lifetime. All the education and learning opportunities he has paid for. He taught kids in Sunday school. He took them on hunting and fishing trips. His actions prove he was the opposite of a pervert. You can't really think that he would *lay his hands* on a child…?"

"I said *child pornography*, not *child molestation* or *rape*. No, I definitely do not think that Jack would 'lay his hands on a child' with the intent to hurt him or her. But we found out that Jack had been systematically abused since he entered the orphanage by both priests and nuns, and—in general—abuse begets abuse. In other words, if someone has been abused as a child, he or she is more likely to abuse others as an adult. We think that Jack sublimated these desires through watching porn.

"Jack could hardly wait to get out of the orphanage and away from his constant molestation, but even after he got out, Sister Mary Delmas pursued him to continue his horror. She could not physically touch him any more but she knew all his triggers. With a word or two, she could dredge up painful memories that almost killed him, and would reduce him to a quivering mass of nerves. It would take days and weeks to get over the nightmares and the accompanying tremors, and his inability to concentrate at work took a toll on his business acumen. Mistakes were made and he had to siphon off bank funds to make restitution for his errors in judgment. Donovan, his confidant, enjoyed watching porn and became Jack's partner in crime. He made Jack's mistakes go away, thus keeping Jack's reputation intact.

"So when Donovan proposed a sure fire deal to Jack that involved only the two of them and had three excellent sources of information in Jack's three friends, Jack listened. It seemed foolproof to him, and in a weird way helped him to channel—and thus alleviate—his painful past. The "deal" was to set up an international child pornography ring via the Internet. Donovan would handle the day-to-day operations, and Jack would make the big decisions utilizing all the information that his three friends dug up regarding online security, how to password-protect, how to make a profit online and what industries or business areas were the most lucrative. Tom, Dan and Bob were clueless as to the product, but they each had agreed to do contract work for a hefty amount of money.

"Donovan and Jack knew that possession of child pornography is a felony under Federal law and in every state. The Federal statutes define *child* as age seventeen or younger. But those viewers who share images (P2P or *peer to peer*) were more likely to have images of very young children, age three or younger, and almost half had images of children that showed sexual violence.

"Donovan is attracted to child porn because it is one of the fastest growing businesses online, with annual revenues of multi-billions. He has a brilliant mind and consequently faces very few mental challenges in life. He was able to pull together and almost launch an incredibly complex, international website that would have made him a multi-billionaire, or so he thought.

"It all started with an online game that Donovan constructed. On the surface, it seemed to be an information site to help the viewer understand the nature of child pornography, giving statistics such as the fact that the United States has more than fifty percent of the volume of international commercialized child porn websites. 'Commercial' refers to distribution for profit; 'non-commercial' is offered free or traded among offenders like the P2P networks. It showed samples of how and what kinds of images were promoted worldwide, and *solicited the help of the viewers to obliterate child porn from online devices.* Through an Internet message board, members of this game shared links to each other's stash of images.

"Donovan planned to be the administrator of this board and had set up an elaborate system of game points where the "players" were shown increasingly graphic child pornography images, cautioning the casual viewer that *these are the images that must be found, reported, and destroyed.* One click shared the awful site with the administrator—Donovan—who then did two things: sent a small credit reward to the player along with a commendation letter, and then erased the viewer's link to his site, making it virtually untraceable.

"In typical Donovan fashion, he felt he had provided work for people all over the world that could not be traced back to him. All sites became the property of the game site, and all connection to the person 'reporting' the site was removed. There was a comment section to be filled out with each 'find', and judging by the nature of the comments, Donovan and his workers would then pursue other pornographic avenues. The supply was endless; the demand overwhelming; the rewards unimaginably lucrative.

"One site called itself *Jalapeno Niños*. The opening page had two words on it, one to the extreme right and one to the extreme left at the top of the page. These were gateway words that took the experienced player in one direction and diverted the novice or inadvertent player away from the site. The words were a variation of "wild" and "mild." *Mild* might show still images of very young children, who were naked, in various poses designed to titillate the adult viewer. *Wild* might show videos of very young children, possibly drugged, being sexually abused by adult males, to the cries of the terrified child's begging them to 'stop'. There might be more sadistic forms of torture as well. Anything to elicit the dominance of the offending male over the submission of the helpless child was fair game, and the more screams, the better. Some scenarios were so heinous that murder was suspected, much like snuff films."

All three adults had tears streaming down their faces. Brian told the girls he was unable to go on talking about it. He said this is a real problem for those FBI agents who worked in the child pornography area. The more proficient they got as investigators who brought the perpetrators to justice, the more exposure they had endured, watching endless hours of gut-wrenching, sadistic torture of innocent children. The abuse is so disturbing that investigators rarely talk about it, even to their spouses.

Suddenly, they all three heard a noise. It was the sound of a key turning in a lock and then in the doorknob itself. The visitor had arrived. Each of the three had chosen a chair to hide behind, out of sight of Jack's office door. When it also was unlocked and the door pushed open, the three held their breaths. Would she see them?

Apparently not.

Sister Mary Delmas went straight to Jack's desk and his computer, turned it on, and went directly to THE FRANCHISE website. It was at this moment that all three stood up and Brian said, "Looking for something, Sister?"

Dolores flipped on the office lights and Brian took a picture of Sister Mary Delmas, hands held up as if to shield her face, before telling her that she was under arrest. She began cursing him and the women, using words most unbecoming of a servant of God. Brian put her hands behind her back and handcuffed her. And then he read her her Miranda rights.

Dolores stood up and looked at Brian. "Before you take her away, I have some things to say." Brian sat down, crossed his arms on his chest and, nodding towards Sister Mary Delmas, said, "Go ahead, Dolores! Fire away!"

Chapter Nineteen

Dolores got up the courage to ask the most important question, "How did Jack and I come to the orphanage in the first place?"

Sister Mary Delmas, faced with exposure and arrest, at first said nothing. Then, "If I cooperate, and tell you what you want to know, will that help me avoid being arrested?"

Brian quickly said "No. But it might help in the length of your sentencing. And I strongly encourage you to cooperate with Dolores because we have only a few minutes before my agents come in here." Brian indicated that Sister Mary Delmas should sit in the visitor chair closest to him. He nodded toward Dolores.

"What do you know about how Jack and I came to the orphanage?"

"Well, the orphanage needed extra funds. We were already getting money from the government for a lot of things and then we found out that that we could get funds for housing mentally ill children. The government would pay $2.25/day per child in mental institutions. But that would involve having inspections as to how the money was being used and for whom. We couldn't afford to have anyone telling us how to train and discipline our charges. We already got a small stipend for each child — $.75/day — from the state for *bona fide* orphans or children who were left to the care of the orphanage. But that was drying up because we were getting so few orphans.

"So we devised a plan whereby we would steal children from their homes and take them to the orphanage where we falsely classified them as orphans. And of course, with you and your brother, we got *two for the money* because your mother was inside your house, washing clothes and she left you and Jack in your backyard where she would be hanging up the clothes. We just came into the back yard, took Jack's hand and your hand and walked to the car and drove away."

"So Jack and I were *not* orphans? We were *stolen* and placed in your orphanage as if we *were* orphans?!!" Dolores started to shake again, enraged. She covered her face with her hands and then launched herself at the nun who had stood up and was doing her best to get out of the way.

Brian stepped in front of Sister Mary Delmas, shielding her from Dolores's onslaught, and grabbed the shrieking Dolores by the arms.

"Dolores. Don't you have some more questions to ask the good nun here? Pull yourself together and get on with it. We only have a little more time left."

Recovering her composure, Dolores had an eerie calm about her and was speaking quietly. "Do you *know* who my parents are? Where do they live?"

Sister Mary Delmas snarled in her direction "Don't you wish you knew, little missy? And aren't you a pretty picture, all painted up like a slut, with your hair curled and dyed like the HARLOTS in the Bible. Well, guess what happened to them, little missy? They were cast into the burning lake of fire that all sinners and perverts will be thrown into, just like YOU, and all of you will burn in Hell for ETERNITY!"

She laughed and laughed, but then started choking and wheezing and coughing. Her eyes were burning and dripping, as was her nose, but she couldn't wipe them because her hands were cuffed. Finally, she stopped making noises and looked up at Dolores.

And then Dolores pointed her finger at the nun, walking in front of her in semi-circles, talking in a singsong voice, laying down a keening sound upon which she threw these words, like curses from a Shakespearean witch.

"Smell the fire, Sister? Want some water, Sister? Soiled yourself, Sister? Hungry, Sister? Want to rest, Sister? Want to be left alone,

Sister? Want the hurting to stop? (Mmmmmmmmmmmmmmm?) YOU will be the one to burn in Hell, not me!"

Then Dolores faced Sister Mary Delmas and said, "Jesus came to my bed one night when I was in the orphanage. I was crying and He told me that one day I would be out of the orphanage, and away from you and the others who hurt me and Jack and the other little children. He said that whatever YOU had done to the other little children would be done to you for Eternity. 'Suffer the little children to come unto me, for of such is the Kingdom of God.' He told me that He would be with me through your last attempts to hurt me and that one day, He and I would expose you and your orphanage torture chamber to the world.

"I was trying to cry without making a noise — oh, yes; remember what happens if you make a noise, Sister? (Dolores assumed a mocking tone.) Why, the nuns will come and make you kneel on the wooden floor in the hallway where everyone can see you, and they will pile big, heavy books on your up-stretched arms, and you will quiver and shake and your knees will soon bleed as bone crushes wood. BUT — if you drop those books, or cry out, or soil yourself, or throw up, well then, you are *taken away*. And YOU — Sister Mary Delmas — (Dolores abruptly stopped in front of Sister Mary Delmas, pointed finger almost touching her nose) and *YOU* know where they are taken — (pointed finger tracing from her forehead down to her nose) — and *you know what happens next*, don't you?"

Sister Mary Delmas had hunched over, looking up into the face of a Dolores she had never before encountered, and recognized a powerful being. She shook her head and tilted her face in Dolores' direction, and responded to Dolores's taunting.

Sister Mary Delmas's eyes glittered with an unholy light and she smiled as she remembered the pleasure she had gotten from their pain. "Yes, yes! I know what happens next! You would be taken to the locked rooms where unspeakable things would be done to you! We sell you miserable children to anyone who has the money and then they can do whatever they want to you! All we ask is a certain charge for a certain amount of time alone with you. And we could sell you over and over again to the highest bidder.

"Each infraction had its own special punishment. I was in charge of fitting the punishment to the crime. I hated children! I still do! They are God's punishment to us for being born in sin. I beat them every chance I got, and I trained the young nuns coming up how to hit the soles of the feet and the elbows because they didn't show bruising so badly.

"I especially hated *bed wetters*! The child who did that had to stand in front of a nun's cell with the soiled linen on his or her head. Your brother Jack was a bed wetter, and I took the greatest pleasure in making sure there was heavy foot traffic across from my cell, with each nun and priest yelling out insults at him as they passed by. "You're no good, Jack me boy!" or "You're a worthless piece of shit." Or "You are just bad, through and through." Or "No wonder your parents sent you here. You were a *mistake* and they had to get rid of you!" Or "You should be ashamed of yourself for being so unworthy of God's love or anyone else's." And the worst taunt of all—"You are so ugly, no one will ever love you!"

Sister Mary Delmas dissolved in croupy laughter, coughing and spitting as pieces of sputum drained down the back of her throat. She was bent over, hands behind her back, peering up with a sideways twist of her head.

"And YOU!" This was directed at Dolores. "You always thought your hair was so beautiful, so perfect. I made the nuns shave your head so that you wouldn't be so fixated on it. You probably think some man is going to come along and think you are beautiful—"

"Stop right there." Dolores held out her hand, palm facing the nun. "I DO have beautiful hair. And I DO have a handsome, rich husband who LOVES ME, despite what you phony-God worshippers put me through!"

Dolores was just drawing a breath to continue her comments when there was a knock on the door and the FBI agents came in and quietly took possession of the nun, who by this time was mumbling incoherently and coughing and laughing hysterically. It was clear that she had gone over the edge, with a little help from her friends.

So it was just Brian, Dolores and Merle again, each quietly reflecting on what had just happened and how it would impact their individual lives. Each knew a crazy chapter in their lives was coming to a close, but exactly HOW that was going to play out was not yet clear. Tomorrow would bring more answers and maybe more problems.

One thing was sure, however. Three people would sleep soundly tonight, by the grace of God. Hallelujah! Amen!

Chapter Twenty

Merle woke to his snoring. Oh, no! We've overslept! Jack will be angry with me, she thought. Then a little voice in her head said,

"Jack's dead, remember? You buried him, had the reading of the will, and with Brian's help, you brought down Jack's international child pornography ring before it launched, remember? So Jack is most definitely NOT the man in bed with you!"

"I am afraid to open my eyes", she whispered to herself. "What if it is Brian?"

And then the kissing began, just the kind she liked. Little butterfly kisses, all over her face and neck. She moaned, reaching out for his—FURRY NECK?

Merle's eyes popped open. And she began to laugh, delighted!

"LUCKY CHARM, you rascal dog! Are you lovin' on mommy? And to think, I almost kissed you back. We've got to do something about that snoring, though."

Lucky Charm was standing over her; intently looking down into her face, tail wagging. Then he jumped off the bed and turned his back to her, signaling that she should follow him to the kitchen, where his food was.

Merle, still laughing, fixed his food and put fresh water in his bowl, and watched as he gulped down the food, drank the water, and looked out the kitchen window, open to the back yard. It was already daylight and looked like the beginning of a bright new day!

Now the obligations of the day were beginning to take shape in her head. Brian had left already, along with the other FBI agents, after they had arrested Sister Mary Delmas and taken her to jail last night. Dolores and her husband Joseph were supposed to come over for breakfast at 9:00, and it was 7:30 now, so she should shower and get to work on their breakfast. But first, a game of ball with Lucky Charm!

As she stood in the kitchen doorway, throwing balls into the back yard and watching Lucky Charm retrieve them, she remembered that Sister Mary Angeline had said she would come over this morning, too. Oh, Goodness! She had better get herself together before her whole morning suddenly came—and *went!*

With Lucky Charm's schedule taken care of, Merle loved on him some more and gently put him in his doggie bed in the laundry room for his three-hour nap. She sometimes forgot that he was just a puppy because he had so much energy! She liked that Lucky Charm gave each phase of his life his absolute total attention and enthusiasm. He did everything full tilt! And now, as she closed the door, she heard the snoring begin — full tilt!

She felt a *frisson* of excitement as she thought of all the options she now had for her future. Whatever choices she made, she was sure they would all be marvelously challenging. After all, she had spent her whole life being taken care of, and she was ready to take care of herself now. She was ready to make her own choices, learning from the disappointments, and joying in getting other things right! She would learn that there were thought processes that worked and thought processes that didn't, but the main thing was to think things out first and then go ahead. It had been a long time since she had had to think, to work things out for herself.

The doorbell rang. Oh, no! Here she was in her bathrobe and slippers with hair that badly needed washing. She was definitely NOT fit company for anyone! Anyone, that is, except the only person in the world who loved her unconditionally, Sister Mary Angeline! "Oh, please let it be her!" she prayed, as she opened the door, cautiously.

There stood Lucille le Vale from *The Bobby Pin Salon*.

"Well, honey! I figured you for an early riser! Good Lord, girl! You need to comb your hair and get some clothes on. What if that cute little FBI agent comes to see you?" And Lucille started laughing, enjoying Merle's red face! "Guess you won't be needing this stuff I brought for you and Dolores, will you? Let's see, I have a bag of goodies for you and one for Dolores and I am taking the *blush* out of your bag…!" and she started laughing again.

"Here, let me pull myself together. I just came by — can't stay — to give you these little basic beauty items you might need along with some little pictures I drew about how to use everything, so you two will look more like *Christmas*, all sparkly! — and not so much like *Halloween*, all scary! I mean it *is paint*, after all!"

She handed the two bags to Merle, who by this time was laughing as well.

"Now you let me know when Dolores comes again — she said it would be about two weeks — and I'll pencil you two girls in together and we will P A R T A Y! See ya!" And she left in a flurry of rubber meeting the road.

"She's right!" thought Merle, as she shut the door. "I *had* better get on with my shower and getting dressed. No telling who will show up next."

But as she headed toward the kitchen, the front doorbell rang, followed by the phone, and then by a knock on the back door.

"Prioritize, Merle, get this in order and you can have it all."
Silently, she followed her own directions by answering the
phone first — "Hello?" — then going to the back door, where
Frances stood and came in as Merle waved her inside. Then
Merle walked to the front door, still waiting on the phone for
the answer to her Hello.

Sister Mary Angeline stood at the front door, a smile on her face.

"Please come in, Sister. Thank you for coming!"

As Merle returned to the phone, Sister Mary Angeline introduced herself to Frances and they stood stiffly, facing each
other. Then Merle saw Frances' face transform from an unchar-
acteristic rigidity to warm smiles as the two women hugged
and sat down to continue talking together.

"Hello?"

"Have things calmed down a little, Merle?"

Instantly, Merle recognized Brian's voice.

"Oh, Brian! It's so good to talk to you again! I thought you had
gone without saying good bye!"

"No, I wouldn't do that. Listen, if you have a minute, I want
you to know that the porn site has been shut down, but we set
it up as a dummy site, so hopefully we will be able to catch

some of the clients that Jack and Donovan planned to entice to the site."

Merle stood, silent. Then, "Is that good?"

"Well, yes. We don't know exactly how Donovan set up the site, but anything we can learn from watching how it works will lead to more arrests and hopefully we will be able to trace the videos and pictures back to where the children are. Then we can arrest their captors and get the children the help they need to function in society."

Merle said, "Brian, can you call me back early this afternoon? I have several people here that I need to talk to and I want to give you my full attention."

"Sure. I have some things to do here at the office before I leave as well, and early afternoon will be fine. What about 2:00?"

"Great! Talk to you then!"

Merle hung up the phone and looked at Sister Mary Angeline and Frances and said, "Listen ladies, I've got to take a shower and get dressed and then I hope you can stay for breakfast. Jack's sister Dolores and her husband Joseph should be here any minute now, and I sure would appreciate it if you all would stay here until I get myself together!"

And with that, she walked down the hall to her bedroom, listening to the lilting laughter of her precious Sister Mary Angeline and the loud happy voice of her neighbor Frances (Lucky Charm's other mother), as they chatted away. Wonder if they would be so happy if they knew what she had to talk with them about? How do you ask your next-to-God-spiritual advisor how to handle the terrible sin she committed when she planned and carried out Jack's death?

As she stepped into the hot shower, she heard snatches of the song, *"What can wash away my sin? Nothing but the blood of Jesus. What can make me whole again? Nothing but the blood of Jesus."*

So Jesus was the Way, but what about the issue of *Intent*?

She washed her face and neck and arms as the words to a proverb flashed in her mind's eye, *"The road to Hell is paved with Good Intentions."* Well, she knew that wanting someone dead wasn't as bad as intending/planning his death, but how did *Intent* figure into what she had accomplished?

She began shampooing her hair. Her shampoo smelled so good, and it made her hair so silky. She began to hum the tune to a song that seemed appropriate, *I'm gonna wash that man right outta my hair — and send him on his way!* Was she singing about Jack? Or Brian?

Jack was already gone. And Brian was leaving. So who was this mysterious man she was thinking about? As she allowed her mind to continue down the path it had started, her imagination took over and she could see a shadowy figure up ahead. And she wondered.

If dogs could turn into humans, what would Lucky Charm look like?

Chapter Twenty-One

Lucille had come and gone, breezing in, bearing gifts. What a great friend she has become, thought Merle. And Sister Mary Angeline, her lifelong friend, was sitting in the kitchen, chatting away with Frances, Merle's newest friend, neighbor and co-mommy to Lucky Charm! She could hear them laugh as she got out of the shower and combed her hair into place. Friends! She never even had ONE before Jack died and now she had four friends!

Looking at the kitchen clock, she temporarily forgot that Dolores and Joseph were coming over for breakfast at 9:00. Oops! It was too close for comfort to the appointed hour! She must hurry now, even though she had pre-cooked most of the breakfast earlier.

Throwing on her sweats, she hurried down the hallway and started to put the rest of her breakfast plans in play. At that very moment, an insistent barking started from the direction of Lucky Charm's bedroom.

"Woof, woof, yourself, you little rascal! Did you come out to be introduced to Mommy's friends? Well, okay. You be a good boy now and I will get you some *foods*." At the sound of that wonderful word, Lucky Charm's tail began to wag furiously, and one could almost see a smile on his doggie face!

Merle handed the squirming puppy to Frances, who said "Oh, Merle, don't bother getting him breakfast. I still have a couple of cans of his food over at my house and since you have more company coming, I will take this sweet angel home with me and feed him and put him to bed for his morning nap. If that's okay with you?"

"Oh, you're a lifesaver, Frances! Thank you so much. I'll call you later this afternoon."

Merle had the coffeepot going and the teapot was boiling, getting hot water ready for whatever caffeine level her guests wanted.

"Come, let me give you a hug, my girl!" Sister Mary Angeline embraced Merle. This was just what a mother's hug should be like, Merle thought.

"Oh, how I have missed your hugs, Sister! And how wonderful it is to have you in my house! Let me fill you in on what's been happening here while we wait on Dolores and her husband Joseph. They should be here in just a few minutes."

Merle started at Jack's death (omitting her applesauce baking spree) and his funeral, and filled Sister Mary Angeline in on all the tragedy-comedy-drama events that had transpired in such a short time, including the events of last night, culminating in the arrest of a *nun* by FBI agents.

As always, Sister Mary Angeline listened intently, but withheld comment until Merle was through.

"Well, my dear, you have certainly come through a very trying time with grace and…maturity, I think. You seem so much more mature than when we last talked. That's what experience does for us, it broadens us in a way no formalized education can. We find out who we truly are when we have been tested in the real world."

"How do you feel about Jack now that he's dead and gone? You know, he just may avoid all the blame and shame that will be heaped on Donovan, even if Donovan tries to smear Jack's good name. And it *is* a good name, Merle. Don't forget all the good that Jack did with his money and his influence. You can be proud of that.

"And what about this FBI agent, Brian? You speak so glowingly of his tactics to prevent this terrible plan from coming to fruition, and the way he treated you as if he really cares about you."

"Sister, Brian is the smartest and most ethical man I know, and he did treat me with care and concern, like you would treat a sister or a very close friend. It felt good to have him in my life for a year, knowing I could talk to him about anything and get his advice about things that were important to me. He never once put me down or made me feel stupid, like Jack did." Merle stared off into the distance, remembering the chair incident, and how utterly demeaned she had felt when Jack called Mr. Simmons to cancel her order.

"Well, is there any love interest with Brian? I mean, as a widow, you are free to date and enjoy the company of men."

"Not with Brian. I don't even know whether or not he is married. But he treated me like a lady and a friend, and I want the relationship we have now to continue."

Merle started moving dishes from the kitchen to the dining room, placing the serving dishes on a table set as if for royalty. "Jack and I had so many lovely gifts for our wedding—china, crystal, silver—and I have never had a chance to use them for *friends* until now," she said.

As Merle started back to the kitchen, Sister Mary Angeline stood up and took her hands and looked intently into her face. "Child, is there anything else you need to tell me before your company comes? It seems as if you are holding something back."

"Uh, not that I can think of, Sister. But I will get in touch with you and let you know if I remember anything."

Just in time, the doorbell rang and there stood a very happy Dolores, with a grinning Joseph by her side.

"Well, you two look mighty happy! Come in and meet my friend, Sister Mary Angeline."

At the name — a nun's name! — Dolores cried out involuntarily "Oh, no! Not another nun!"

There was dead silence. Then suddenly, Sister Mary Angeline said "I get that all the time!" and she started giggling. Merle, flustered, began to laugh nervously, then enthusiastically. Joseph doubled over, laughing and saying "Hey, Lawdy!" like he always did when he got nervous. So naturally, Dolores had to laugh as well. Tears were running down all their faces, when Dolores got hiccups. Eventually, Dolores, apologizing for her hiccups, shook hands with Sister Mary Angeline, followed by Joseph, and then they all sat down to eat Merle's Magnificent Meal!

Chapter Twenty-Two

"Well, Merle, what are you going to do next?" Joseph, who hardly ever spoke, raised the question that was on everyone's mind. "Sell the house? Travel? What?"

Merle had finished taking the empty dishes back to the kitchen, and now everyone was relaxing at the table with cookies and coffee and tea.

"I'm thinking of going to college," Merle said.

"Wonderful, my girl!" said Sister Mary Angeline.

"A worthy goal," said Joseph.

"But, why?" said Dolores. "Honey, with all your money you could travel the world! Buy clothes and jewelry! Get a condo in New York and another one in L.A. and go back and forth! You can't be serious about going to *college*!"

"Well, I am going to look into it and see what I want to do with a college degree. If I can achieve my goals without going the academic route, then I will look into some other way."

"What *are* your goals?" said Sister Mary Angeline. "I know at the orphanage, you were a person who could quietly console, or uplift, or inspire whatever was needed for a person at the time. You were an enabler of the best kind because although you could encourage people, you could also move them to take action. And you were a realist, not an idealist. So you were able to give hope to those around you, not false hope, but real insight that you saw in the people you wanted to help. You seemed to be able to *see into* a person — to see what they could be and do, and not just what they or their circumstances presented to the world."

Merle said, "Sister, I have been a prisoner in a golden cell — well-fed, treated with deference, most of my earthly wants and needs provided immediately. But I *meant* nothing as a person. I *did* nothing as a person. I *helped no one* as a person. And I was *so lonely*! Until Brian came, I had no one to discuss ideas with. I didn't realize until Jack died that everyone in this town could name Jack's three best friends, but most people didn't even know he was married much less what my name was. Even the minister failed to acknowledge me as Jack's wife. I felt *invisible*..."

There was an awkward silence.

"And then, I fell in love with someone who loved me back unconditionally, not for whose wife I was, or how much I had, or what I looked like! And I felt *euphoric!* (She looked at Sister Mary Angeline, questioningly.) Is that the right word, Sister?"

Sister Mary Angeline's face was beaming! "Yes, my child! *Euphoria* is feeling great happiness or great wellbeing. But who *is* this person? I've never even heard you allude to anyone of this magnitude."

"It doesn't matter *who* he is. What matters is that when he came into my life, I realized that I was capable of great depths of feeling that I had never before encountered! Suddenly, someone I cared for loved *me!* Just *as* I was, just *who* I was. And I wanted to share that feeling of being loved with the world! With *everyone* in the world!

"But I realized that in order to be my best self, I had to challenge every part of me; how I look, how to learn things beyond my own interests, things that can help others; how to interact with others through humor and concern and information. How to become *wise*...

"And, thanks to Lucille, I now know how to look my best! And because she sees different sides of me, she can help me present my best self to the world in any situation. Thanks to her, I was perceived as being serious yet attractive at the reading of Jack's will. She has already shown me a 'look' for being academically serious, yet approachable. She has shown me possibilities that I could never see in my mirror.

"Remember at the orphanage, Sister? I wasn't really interested in a whole lot of things, and I chose as my friends those girls who shared my interests. Well, now I want to try a lot of different things to be able to feel what others are feeling—what's that called, Sister?"

"*Empathy*, dear child! Being able to understand what others are experiencing."

"And I wanted to be able to be silly, or happy, or snicker at the least little thing! I wanted to feel…what is it, Sister, that wells up inside a person that makes you giggle and laugh that is so cleansing, and so mood-altering?"

"*Joy! That's joy!* Oh, my blessed child! The Lord has given you a great task! You will bring Love and Joy and Understanding to God's people wherever you are on this Earth!"

Joseph had quietly placed his hand over Dolores's hand.

Dolores said, "I envy you, Merle. You may not know exactly what you want to do or where you want to do it, but you sure do know who you want to do it with!"

Silence.

Sister Mary Angeline cleared her throat. "With whom you want to do it, Dolores."

And then she giggled, and laughter flew all around the table!

Dolores looked at Sister Mary Angeline and said, "I don't believe you're a real nun. I mean I *know* you are, but I never saw any nuns like you in our orphanage. All they wanted to do was to hurt us and humiliate us kids. There wasn't any love there. There were no friendships; nobody helped anybody. We each just tried to survive the best we could. There was no encouragement or any teaching or training. I mean, when you corrected me just then, I had no idea what I was supposed to have said, but I will remember the correct usage now because you cared enough about me to teach me. And then, too, I love how you giggle!"

"Dolores, even though I never met you until today, Merle has told me of the difficult upbringing that you and Jack experienced. May I now consider you my child, just as I consider Merle my child? I want you to know that Sister Mary Delmas was an *aberration*, a departure from the norm, who in no way represents the presence of God in women who choose to serve Him as nuns. I want to offer my services to you to talk any time of the night or day about anything that comes into your mind or your life that reminds you of your torment. You can recover from a lot of these memories, and you can learn methods of dealing with the triggers that set them off. All my numbers are listed inside this packet I am giving you. So call me any time.

"Remember, *evil people always are damaged people*. The more evil they exhibit, especially to those under their influence or control, the more damage their souls have been subjected to. These people have not been loved and therefore are without God. They are literally, *God-less*. Ordinary people cannot hope to stand against them without the presence of God in their lives. But sometimes we can do extraordinary things if we have been practicing one thing, Love. We have only one definition of God and that is, *God is Love*.

"To love is not easy. It demands everything within us to constantly be at attention and to seek out those who need our love the most. We all have the seeds of Love within us and Love can grow at any time. But we have to nurture it, feed and water it, and constantly check two things.

"First, is what I did or am thinking of doing the *Loving* thing to do? If we choose Love every time, then Love becomes our default position and we grow in Love. Second, we must honor the good sense that God gave us. We must hone the skill of *discernment*, the process of exhibiting keen insight and good judgment, to advance God's goals through us. We don't need to be viewed as the nutcase who stands on a street corner and yells out 'God loves you!' That only serves to bring attention to our selves. But to seek out those in need every day while simultaneously developing our own radar beacon, well, that takes commitment and focus and purpose! And that is no job for sissies!"

Merle said, "I don't believe I have ever heard the term 'Radar Beacon', Sister. What is it?"

"Let me give you the dictionary definition. "*A Radar Beacon is a fixed device that sends or receives, or amplifies, alters, and returns a radar signal, permitting a distant receiver to determine its bearing.*" In other words, it is a *booster*. We are the beacons and God's Love is the signal.

"I think God has chosen some of us to function in this way to participate in a gigantic communication community that can accomplish far more together than any one of us can. We must seek out, identify, and align with those other 'beacons' so that God's great work can be accomplished on an incredible scale!"

Sister Mary Angeline reached in her rather large handbag, which she had put at her feet when they came to the table, pulled out a couple of large manila envelopes and laid them on the table in front of her.

"You girls are living in wonderful times! Even though the world as we know it may seem to be crumbling around us, there are miracles zipping through the ether, swirling around our heads and piercing our hearts as surely as well-aimed arrows! It will soon be made known to you—and to me—what our part will be in bringing these miracles to fruition.

"I have proof of this and I am sharing that proof with you (giving each girl an envelope) because you are going to be doing great things! When you read what is inside these envelopes, you will have a clearer idea of what God wants *you* to do, so read these few pages with an open mind and a searching heart. You have each other to lean on and to talk to and to encourage. And Dolores, you have Joseph, whom I believe to be a Godsend, to help you not only through the rest of your life, but also to help you *enjoy* the rest of your life! You both have money, management skills, and the ability to see the magic in others! You literally *can* make dreams come true!

"You each knew Jack as a troubled soul who struggled every day with demons we can't imagine, but who was actively nurturing the Godbits that were in him, and who was making a positive difference at the time of his death. Be proud of the man that he was struggling so hard to become, and help his dreams come true. Those dreams are outlined in his will and now that Donovan is out of the picture, someone is needed to take ownership of those dreams and activate them. Use your money and your time and your presence to stir them up, pour them out on people who have never even dared to dream, and then stand back and watch what happens!"

Merle and Dolores and even Joseph had stars in their eyes! What a motivational speaker this little nun was!

Clearing his throat, Joseph said, "I hate to break this up, ladies, but Dolores and I have a plane to catch, so we need to be going."

"Oh, no! Wait just one more minute! Dolores, I must ask you about Jack's allergy to apples..." Merle was stopped by the puzzled look on Dolores's face.

"His allergy to...Oh, my gosh! He told you he was *allergic* to apples?"

"Yes, and I had to be so careful not to buy anything that might have any part of the apple in it because he said he might die if he ate apples."

"Jack never had an allergy to apples. He didn't like the taste of apples, especially the pithy ones, but when the nuns told him he *had* to 'eat an apple a day to keep the doctor away', he saw his opportunity to control a little piece of his world and he took it! You see, if any kid got sick, the local doctor would be called in, and if a kid died, well then there would be an investigation and the orphanage would be under scrutiny from the State from then on. But was he *allergic* to apples? No."

Merle was speechless. Only she knew the full impact of Dolores's words on her future.

The only thing she could think of was a quote from Sir Walter Scott, "Oh, what a tangled web we weave, when first we practice to deceive."

But Sir Walter Scott's murders were plotted and carried out *in a book*. Jack's "murder" had been plotted in church, the "murder" weapon had been fashioned in Jack's kitchen and what was supposed to be the "murder" had taken place in Jack's easy chair in front of the fireplace in Jack's own den. What part of all these decisions that Merle had made would Sister Mary Angeline say was the *Loving* decision?

Chapter Twenty-Three

J oseph and Dolores took their leave from Merle's house with hugs all around, promising to see Merle in about two weeks, "and you, too, Sister, if you are available!" As Dolores gave an extra hug to the nun, the Sister told her to read up on the things that were in the envelope that she had given to both Merle and Dolores. "There might be a test," she said solemnly. And then — *wait for it* — they all dissolved in laughter!

"You, too, my darling daughter!" said Sister Mary Angeline, when she and Merle were finally alone. "There are massive changes being brought about in the Catholic Church, and I want you to see the direction in which the church is going. It is truly exciting!"

Sister Mary Angeline took the envelope out of Merle's hands and opened it up. She took out three stapled sets of papers and began reading the contents to Merle, adding comments to let her know what the writers of each article were trying to get across to the lay people, those who were not Catholic as well as those who were.

"We in the Church had been hearing bits and pieces of what kind of leader Pope Francis would be. But we couldn't believe what we were hearing! His spoken words and the words printed about him were so different from those of previous Popes that we first thought it was the usual PR stuff that is put out when a new pope is elected. But later, as the Pope became more sure of sharing his real thoughts and feelings with the world, we realized that something highly unusual was developing before our very eyes!

"I got so excited when I tried to share my perception of who the new Pope is and what he is trying to achieve, that I feared I was saying what *I* wanted to hear! *But actions speak much louder than words!* So I decided to wait a few months and see the consistency — or the inconsistencies — between what this new pope says and how he acts.

"Then on July 29, 2013, Rachel Donadio wrote an article in *The New York Times* entitled *"On Gay Priests, Pope Francis Asks, 'Who Am I to Judge?'"* Quoting many European interviews during the past five months, Donadio points out how the 'dominant Catholic story is (becoming) *'Charismatic Pope Takes World by Storm.' If someone is gay and he searches for the Lord and has good will, who am I to judge?"* Donadio said that the fact that the Pope made such comments, albeit in Italian, making a point of using the English word *gay,* was revolutionary!

The new Pope also told reporters that he 'sought a *theology of women* and a greater role for them in Catholic life', and said that he felt he was elected for his belief 'that the Catholic Church must engage in dialogue with the *world*—even with those it disagrees with—if it wants to stay vibrant and relevant.'

Laying down the first document, Sister Mary Angeline picked up the second set of pages. Claudio Lavanga, an NBC News correspondent, wrote from Vatican City, "*Vatican sets up special committee on child sex abuse.*"

"The Vatican is to set up a special committee to improve measures to protect children against sexual abuse within the Church", said the Archbishop of Boston, Cardinal Sean Patrick O'Malley.

"The commission, named a month after the pope's election, underlined his (Pope Francis's) determination to push through reforms of the Vatican's top heavy administration and tackle festering scandals like the issue of sexual abuse of children by priests. In essence, this new committee will be faced with the difficult task of re-establishing faith in the Church's ability to tackle evil from within."

Sister Mary Angeline gave the packet back to Merle.

"Oh, Sister! This truly sounds like a new day for the church, doesn't it? I thank you so much for these articles, which I will read, hungrily! Did you read the *Text of Pope Francis's Christmas Message?* It was like reading poetry! I made a copy for you after I heard it! Listen to these key points:

§   *"I take up the song of the angels who appeared to the shepherds in Bethlehem on the night when Jesus was born.*

§   *I ask everyone to share in this song, for every man or woman who keeps watch through the night, who hopes for a better world, who cares for others while humbly seeking to do his or her duty.*

§   *Today I voice my hope that everyone will come to know the true face of God, the Father, who has given us Jesus. My hope is that everyone will feel God's closeness, live in his presence, love him and adore him.*

§   *Never lose the courage of prayer! We have seen how powerful prayer is! And I am happy today, too, that the followers of different religious confessions are joining us in our prayer for peace.*

§   *Looking at the Child in the manger, our thoughts turn to those children who are the most vulnerable victims of wars, and we think too of the elderly, the battered women, and the sick. Yet you, Lord, forget no one!*

§   *Let us allow our hearts to be touched! Let us allow ourselves to be warmed by the tenderness of God; we need his caress. God is full of love! God is peace! Let us ask him to help us to be peacemakers each day, in our lives, in our families, in our cities and nations, in the whole world!"*

Finally, an inclusive Leader at the head of the Church, thought Merle.

190

"Sister, I feel so hopeful now! I have gone from not having any hope at all to having all these amazing choices! I truly feel excitement where I felt fear and agitation. I didn't know whom to trust and now I am surrounded by new and old friends who are truly concerned with my wellbeing. I am so blessed!"

"And yet..." Sister Mary Angeline looked searchingly into Merle's eyes. Merle looked away.

"See! That's the look you had as a small child when you were wrestling with something."

"Well, you are right, as usual, and I *am* 'wrestling' with a problem that only I can work out. For many reasons I cannot discuss this with anyone just yet. Sorry!"

"Well, my girl, I am as close as your phone, so call me any time of the night or day. But I do encourage you to get this thing resolved as soon as possible. You know, constant anxiety feels as if the flesh is being shredded from our spiritual bones. Intense pain makes us unable to think rationally, and all we want to do is dig a hole and hide in it until the pain goes away. Our vulnerability makes us clutch at anything that will make the pain subside.

"But until you search, diligently, for the cause of that pain, no progress will be made, no resolution will be achieved. You look weary from worrying, from thinking, from going over and over the same thing without reaching resolution or enlightenment or a different perspective.

"The soul can suffer many things, but it must be revitalized or we become damaged as people."

Sister Mary Angeline turned away from Merle, picked up her large purse and headed for the door.

"Thank you, sister. I will think about what you have said and I will call you next week to get together again."

"And, Merle—I want you to tell me who this man is who has brought Love into your heart, and I want to meet him, soon."

As the door closed, Merle sighed. "I wonder if she would think I am totally crazy to be in love with, and loved by, my dog, Lucky Charm. I think God sent him to me to train me in the care and feeding and loving of a future *human* love interest!"

Merle's head was aswirl with thoughts, chief among which was the word INTENT.

"I planned a murder and carried it out. That's *intent*.

"My plan worked. Jack died. As a result of *intent*.

"No one knows of my plan. Of my *intent*.

Chapter Twenty-Three

"I chose a weapon that was truly untraceable. By *intent*.

"The weapon turned out to not be deadly, but he died anyway. Through *intent*.

"My new life is wonderful! As a result of *intent*.

"I tried to confess to Sister Mary Angeline but it didn't feel right. Maybe I should tell Brian?

"NO!!" She almost yelled this out loud.

The answer was so instantaneous and so loud that it surprised her! She most definitely didn't want Brian to know that she was not only capable of planning and carrying out a murder, she was in no way remorseful. And don't you have to be remorseful to be forgiven?

And to whom could she confess her sin and be forgiven of it?

Chapter Twenty-Four

It seemed to Merle that there was no one to talk to about her highly successful plan to murder Jack. So much good had come of his death that she just couldn't feel remorseful, but increasingly she felt the need for forgiveness. God's forgiveness.

And she needed to talk out what she had done with someone who could help her understand exactly what had happened. It was as if she had pointed a gun, loaded with blanks, at someone, pulled the trigger and killed them, only to find out that they had died of *fright* and not of a bullet wound. The person was dead all right, which is what she intended, but how much guilt should she feel? How much responsibility should she bear? How much forgiveness should she ask for? And from whom should she ask this forgiveness?

A priest could forgive her. But she wasn't Catholic. Would that matter? Maybe Sister Mary Angeline could tell her, but she was astute enough to figure out that Merle was more involved in Jack's death than she had imagined and also she might lose respect for Merle by acting in such an intentional way. Merle didn't want to take the chance.

Brian? No, his respect was even more important to Merle than Sister Mary Angeline's. She definitely couldn't even bring up the subject with him. He might think her just a common murderer—murderess? And knowing his belief system and his ethical commitment, he would turn her in and let the courts decide her fate.

If only she could talk to someone *in private*.

And then it came to her. What was more private than the Internet?

She ran back to her bedroom, got her laptop and keyed in the words "Will God Forgive Murderers?" And there she read that there is only one 'unforgivable sin' and that is to not acknowledge Jesus Christ as God's son. Every thing else is forgivable!

Wow!

She read on, *"It is impossible for a Christian to commit an unpardonable sin. Once you receive Christ's atonement, sin is no longer able to separate you from God."*

"The Holy Spirit says that murdering someone is a sin. You need to agree with this. Step one is you agree with God that what you did was wrong. The second step is to turn away from sin in your heart

by wanting God to have his way with your life. You can either have a distant relationship with God or a close relationship with God. At any moment in time, your soul either cares about pleasing God or it does not. Whenever it does, you are in alignment with God. God's approval is extremely important to you.

"Is that where you are now? If so, then you are pleasing God."

"Repentance is the solution for murdering someone. Once you repent and return to earnestly wanting to please God, then all is well between you and Him. At that point, there might be something specific that He wants you to do about the fact that you've killed someone. Only you will know what God is asking you to do. You need to back off and let God clean up the mess you've made. He's the only One who knows how."

Merle's eyes were glued to the computer screen, fingers poised above the keys. Oh, how she wished that a real priest would appear and tell her that her sin was forgiven! Her fingers typed in "Confession of Sin to a Priest." A paragraph grabbed her heart. *"It requires humility to confess your sins. It also gives great peace to hear the priest say 'In Jesus' name I absolve you from your sins in the name of the Father and of the Son and of the Holy Spirit.'"*

Merle repeated these words out loud. And then she said them again, louder! "I am *forgiven*! If God can forgive a murderer, He can certainly forgive an almost-murderer! And He can forgive *Intent*!"

God forgives me of my sin!"

And her trembling fingers typed in "Forgiveness of Sins", and there was even more good news!

"Repentance is the key to being forgiven."

"If you can confess it, you can be forgiven of it!"

"There is no sin too great for God to forgive!"

"You are a new creation…so forget your past! As a child of God, your past has been wiped away, and you are given a fresh start!"

"When your sins are forgiven, they are removed from you as far as the east is from the west!"

"We are told not to look at the past, but to press forward towards the future. God wants us to forgive ourselves and allow Jesus to clean our conscience from all the evil we have done."

And then, Merle clicked on the next site, *The Pursuit of God*, "Serious Topics for Serious Christians", which started out with these words. "How to use this site: Our goal is to help you grow in your relationship with God."

As she scrolled down past the various topics, she came to the last one, "Remember Where Truth Comes From," and read,

"Truth comes from God, not from an Internet site. Always pray before, during, and after you read any information on this site. The Holy Spirit is the only Teacher you can trust. Ask Him to give you discernment as you read and to show you how to properly apply any truth that you come across. Don't ever trust a human to properly convey God's truth to you. If you read something on this site that makes you feel inspired about your walk, then give (God) the glory, not us."

Merle could not explain the joy she felt! Suddenly she knew how blessed she was! She had a reason—many reasons—to live! She had Jack's money to honor his memory with, to honor the Godbits that Jack possessed but did not know how to use. And she would spend the rest of her life using her past experiences, and her money, and her desire to please God to bring as much joy and happiness and relief to her little corner of the world as possible. She had friends and family to love and laugh with, and her precious Lucky Charm for comic relief and unconditional love!

Now she was eager to see Brian this afternoon! And she would welcome seeing Sister Mary Angeline who could be quite useful in helping Merle make her life plans. Oh, the *Joy* of it all! The endless opportunities that stretched out before her!

Where would her life go next?

THE END

CPSIA information can be obtained
at www.ICGtesting.com
Printed in the USA
FFOW03n0117281016
28853FF